THE

Traveler's

HANDBOOK

& OTHER TALES

BEDTIME BUDDHA

THE *Astral Traveler's* HANDBOOK

& OTHER TALES

DAVID MICHIE

CONCH

CONCH BOOKS

CONCH

Conch Books, an imprint of Mosaic Reputation Management (Pty) Ltd

Cover/book design: Sue Campbell Book Design
Cover photo: Pono Lopez (milky way)
Author photo: Janmarie Michie
Proofreading: www.donnahillyer.com

Cataloguing-in-Publication details are available from the National Library of Australia www.trove.nla.gov.au

ISBN: 978-0-9944881-6-9 (Print USA version)
ISBN: 978-0-9944881-7-6 (e-book USA version)

DAVID MICHIE

With his customary lightness of touch David Michie presents charming and evocative Buddhist tales, that will both delight and instruct. A gift of a book—guaranteed to produce sweet dreams.

—VICKI MACKENZIE, Author of *Cave In the Snow* and *The Revolutionary Life of Freda Bedi*

David Michie is an enchanting storyteller and Bedtime Buddha is a collection of stories that will surprise and delight. Each story frames an imagined realm, circle of friends, or an adventure holding a pearl of great wisdom waiting to be discovered. A must read that aptly balances entertainment and enlightenment!

—PAUL SWANSON, Host of the *Contemplify* Podcast

I am always in awe of David Michie's talent to weave such powerful wisdom into his books; yet still be entertaining on so many levels. Bedtime Buddha stories will have you dreaming with such amazing energy that you will awake in the morning with peaceful yet a positive outlook on your day ahead. Congratulations David on another fabulous series!

—TARA TAYLOR, International Intuitive, Spiritual Teacher, and Best Selling Author

David has written this series of enchanting tales to warm the heart and soul before bedtime. Each story is peppered with subtle gems of wisdom that will help any modern-day seeker upgrade their life for a more meaningful and purposeful existence.

—ZOË B, Founder of Simple Life Strategies

David Michie is the author of *The Dalai Lama's Cat* series, *The Queen's Corgi: On Purpose* and *The Magician of Lhasa*, as well as several works of non-fiction. He is also the founder of Mindful Safaris to Africa.

www.davidmichie.com

ALSO BY DAVID MICHIE

Fiction
The Dalai Lama's Cat
The Dalai Lama's Cat and The Art of Purring
The Dalai Lama's Cat and The Power of Meow
The Magician of Lhasa
The Queen's Corgi: On Purpose

Bedtime Buddha Series
The Astral Traveler's Handbook & Other Tales

Non-fiction
Buddhism for Busy People
Hurry Up and Meditate
Enlightenment to Go
Why Mindfulness is Better than Chocolate
Buddhism for Pet Lovers

CONTENTS

FOREWORD

BY THE DALAI LAMA'S CAT

THE IDEA CAME ABOUT ONE GORGEOUS HIMALAYAN MORNING. I WAS sitting in my favorite spot—the first-floor windowsill of the Dalai Lama's meeting room. It is here that I like to spend my days basking in the sunshine, keeping an eye on the courtyard below, while eavesdropping on all the intriguing goings-on within.

That particular morning, His Holiness's visitor was one of the most influential movie directors in Hollywood. Being a cat of great discretion, dear reader, I'm afraid I can't possibly tell you who he was. But I am willing to give you a few tiny hints.

If you have ever felt your compassion aroused by an extra-terrestrial being, perhaps, or marveled at a theme park filled with dinosaurs, or been enthralled by adventures involving ancient civilizations, it is just possible that you may be able to guess the identity of this person. You know, the fellow with the beard and glasses. Yes, *him*!

For a while I'd been in that delightful semi-sleep state, dreaming and softly purring while the conversation inside wafted over me. The two men had been talking about the power of language to transport us to places we could never otherwise go, the visitor noting that certain words and phrases were especially evocative. Which was when I heard him say, "The four most magical words in the English language."

At once, my whiskers tingled. We Tibetan Buddhists are keen on magical words and the famous director was evidently about to reveal some special incantation. Four words which, in the mind of the listener, would change all that followed.

In the very next moment, however, I guessed exactly what he was about to say. The four words came to me, without even having to think. That was because I heard them night and day, chanted with great devotion by monks and Western visitors alike: *Om mani padme hum.*

The mantra was an evocation of love and compassion. When repeated, with deepening understanding and conviction, those four words could most certainly be said to have a magical effect, even if not an immediate one.

As I caught the scent of Himalayan pine, wafting on a pristine breeze from the ice-capped mountains, I thought how lucky I was to know such things, and to be a cat of such very deep wisdom.

The conversational pause inside the room seemed to go on forever. On the brink of revealing the invocation of magical power, the director evidently knew how to draw out the suspense. Even though I knew exactly what he was about to reveal, I still wanted him to reveal it!

Which was when he came out with something utterly unexpected. Four words, quite frankly, I would never have even guessed.

"Once upon a time," said he.

Lifting my head, I turned to look at him directly. Had the man taken leave of his senses?!

"Once upon a time?" repeated His Holiness.

It was only when the Dalai Lama said it, in that gentle, melodious voice of his, that I realized. Ah! Four words in the *English* language. I supposed that was different.

"There are equivalents in many other languages," continued the visitor, to my further disgruntlement. "The Germans have '*es war einmal*,' and the French '*Il était une fois*.' You find it in many cultures going back in time, like Chinese and even Sanskrit."

Oh really? This was the first I'd heard of it.

"And why are these words magical?" asked His Holiness.

Exactly what I was wondering. Why indeed?

"Because we learn them as children at the beginning of magical tales. We associate them with opening our imagination to limitless possibilities. As adults, those four words give us permission to suspend our judgment, to let go of ordinary convention. To become child-like again."

His Holiness was sitting up in his chair. And I have to say, dear reader, that I, too, raised myself up from the windowsill and turned around, so intrigued was I by what the director was saying.

"When we are child-like," the Dalai Lama observed, "we become more open."

His visitor was nodding.

"We learn in different ways."

"Right brain," agreed the other. "The level of creativity and intuition."

"In Tibetan Buddhism—" His Holiness leaned forward in his chair "—this is considered most important."

"It's also," ventured the visitor, "the reason I like to ask: why does it stop?"

"Stop?" queried the Dalai Lama.

"When we grow up. There are no more tales of enchantment. No more "Once upon a time" stories. But it seems to me that, as adults, we need these more than ever!"

I liked what the visitor was saying so much that I hopped off the sill, padded across a finely woven, ornate, Indian rug, and approached where he was sitting.

It seemed that the Dalai Lama liked it too. He was smiling in agreement. "Spiritual teachers in all traditions use stories to convey insights. Deeper wisdom. Stories can do things that debate and logic cannot. They can touch mind, and also—" he lifted his right hand to his chest "—heart."

"The power of parables," concurred his visitor.

His Holiness ventured further. "And the time of day we tell such stories is also important. They can have a big impact if we hear them just before going to sleep. By focusing the mind on positive things, we can transform sleep, which is a neutral activity, into something very useful."

"Making a virtue of a necessity?" suggested the director.

"Exactly!" he beamed.

When he speaks, the Dalai Lama often uses just a few words to convey meaning that can be understood on many different levels. From other conversations I'd overhead in the past, I knew that the "something very useful", he mentioned, by which people could transform their sleep, was an important and fascinating subject.

His Holiness's expression changed, lines appearing on his forehead. "These days, before people go to sleep, there's too much of this." He mimicked someone keying words into a mobile device. "Great agitation. So I agree, there is a great need for bedtime stories." He gestured his visitor in acknowledgement. "Especially for grown-ups!" he added.

Both men laughed.

I chose this moment to hop up onto the visitor's lap, taking him by surprise.

"How delightful!" He took in my charcoal face, big blue eyes and luxuriant, cream-colored coat—the markings of we, Himalayan cats.

"I didn't know you had a cat?" The director was not the first visitor to have made such an observation. And as I've noted before, why should the Dalai Lama *not* have a cat—if "having a cat" is an accurate description of the relationship.

I circled on his lap, trying to decide exactly where I would position myself. As I did, His Holiness said, "As you can see, she is not a creature of fiction."

The visitor glanced in the direction from which I'd come, realizing that I must have been sitting nearby all along. As I settled onto his knees, he said, "I am sure she must hear many enchanting tales, sitting on the windowsill."

"Oh yes," agreed the Dalai Lama. "She could share some wonderful stories."

In the days that followed, whether dozing on the sill, or being pampered downstairs in the kitchen by the executive chef, Mrs. Trinci, I would sometimes recollect that conversation: Once upon a time. Transform sleep into something useful.

And it was true, I thought—I did hear many fascinating tales. Some were stories of mystical yogis and monks in the Himalayas. Others involved middle-aged women or inquiring young men in the West. The most precious of these stories, just like the fables of old, contained some transformative insight, some life-affirming wisdom, that touched not only the mind, but also the heart.

But where to start?

If I have learned anything living with His Holiness, dear reader, it is the simple truth that if you need help with something, *anything*, the first step is to ask. Whether it is a lip-smacking serving of Mrs. Trinci's finest diced chicken liver, or the inspiration of the Buddhas when embarking on some new creative project, we are surrounded by beings whose only wish is to see us happy and fulfilled and, most especially, to help us offer happiness and fulfillment to others. Sometimes these beings may be seen. Sometimes unseen. In my own case, I only need to be in the same room as the Dalai Lama and I am touched by his benevolent inspiration.

Mulling over the matter of bedtime stories, for a period of quite some weeks after that visit by the Hollywood director, a curious thing happened. Perched on the end of His Holiness's bed as he lifted a text to read before lights out, he would look down towards me, and perhaps reach out to deliver a reassuring stroke. And as he did, without any effort on my own part, a memory would surface of a visitor who had come to share a particular story, one that would occupy my imagination as I went to sleep that night, and would be perfect to include in a collection of tales for grown-ups.

Why those stories arose at that particular time, and whether or not they were a product of the Buddha's inspiration is something I will leave to you to decide. Soon you will be as familiar with the people and their stories as I am, dear reader, because they are the stories you now hold in your hands.

So, if you will allow me a suggestion, instead of going to bed with your mobile device tonight, why not leave that source of agitation in another room, and take this book with you instead? Along, perhaps, with a throat-warming mug of cocoa or lemon tea? Summon your fur babies to join you, so they can tune in too, and leave yourself plenty of time—I feel sure that once you have embarked on one of the nugget-sized tales shared on the following pages, you will not want to leave it until you have read it all the way through.

At which point, without entirely leaving the world of each story behind you, bid goodnight to your loved ones, turn out the light, and allow your imagination to remain in the place and time evoked by the tale.

All that remains, dear reader, is for me to offer you the following Tibetan Buddhist blessing: may you have good sleep, auspicious dreams, and may you taste the true nature of reality.

Om mani padme hum!

THE TALE OF THE TOOTHLESS OLD PEASANT

Once upon a time an old peasant man called Yonten lived alone in a remote valley of Ladakh, Northern India. No one knew much about Yonten. He wasn't connected to any of the dozen families who had smallholdings in the Nala valley. Nor was he attached to the monastery at the top of the mountain. Yonten kept himself to himself, living in his two-roomed hut, tending to his small herd of yaks and goats, and growing barley and potatoes, as was the custom in that part of the world.

Yonten was rarely seen by the locals or the monks, and never invited to join them for a meal or social occasion. This wasn't only because of his well-known self-sufficiency; it was also because his was not a face you wanted at your table.

An old man—just how old, nobody knew—he had long since lost all the teeth in his mouth, giving his face a caved-in look. His eyes were rheumy. Hair sprouted from his ears in unsightly profusion. Local families and monks kept their distance, their main form of contact being an arm wave from afar—usually towards the great, slanting boulder on the mountainside, beneath which Yonten often sat for protection from the elements, watching over his livestock.

The only thing that everyone knew about Yonten was that whenever they saw him, day or night, and no matter what else he was doing at the time, he was always spinning his prayer wheel while reciting the mantra of Chenrezig, the Buddha of Compassion: *Om mani padme hum. Om mani padme hum.*

Yonten, like many who lived in the remote mountains, was illiterate. He knew nothing about the Buddha of Compassion apart from what he could remember learning at the feet of his guru, Lama Palden. And he didn't remember much.

He did know that Chenrezig was the embodiment of the compassion of all the Buddhas. That his radiant white color symbolized purity and power. That, as a consequence, repeating his mantra purified one's mind and accumulated limitless virtue, thereby awakening one's own Buddha nature. Most especially, he remembered Lama Palden telling him that if he recited Chenrezig's mantra enough, the merit created would be sufficient for him to perceive Chenrezig's Pure Land directly for himself.

Lama Palden had been the last abbot of Nala Monastery. He had died thirty years ago, following which the monastery had gone into a gradual decline, its numbers dwindling to just nine remaining monks, none of whom felt qualified to offer teachings.

So inspiring had Lama Palden been as a teacher, and so unshakable was Yonten in his devotion as a student that, thirty years after his death, Yonten was still doing exactly as his lama had instructed him—reciting the mantra of the Buddha of Compassion at every opportunity.

In the three decades since Lama Palden's demise, a handful of lamas had visited Nala Monastery to offer blessings and teachings for the benefit of both the monks as well as the local people. Yonten would always attend these occasions, sitting at the very back of the small gompa.

Every two years or so, when a high lama was visiting the nearest significant monastery, Hemis, a full day's hike away, the monks would lead a small group of locals along the mountains. They would stay at Hemis overnight, attending teachings and ceremonies the following day.

Accommodation at Hemis was limited, which meant that so, too, was the size of the group that could travel there. Visits to Hemis were festive occasions, and because the monks at the local monastery came from families along the valley on whose support they depended, it was always family members who were chosen to accompany them.

On visit after visit, hearing that a trip to Hemis was in the offing, Yonten would present himself at the monastery door and request, with the utmost humility, to be allowed to join the group. On several such occasions, it had been the Dalai Lama himself who had visited Hemis. Like many Tibetan Buddhists, Yonten considered His Holiness to be an emanation of Chenrezig, the Buddha whose mantra he so constantly recited. He believed that the chance to catch even a glimpse of this holy being in the flesh represented the most precious experience to which he could aspire.

Well before these visits, when he went up to the monastery doors, requesting to join the group visiting Hemis, Yonten would undertake three, full-length prostrations to whoever he beseeched.

"If you would kindly permit me to join you on this visit," Yonten would beg Kalsang, the only monk known to have read every book at Nala Monastery, "I could go to Chenrezig Pure Land a happy man."

Kalsang would tell Yonten that his request would be considered—alongside that of many other requests received from his neighbors along the valley.

"If you would kindly permit me to join you on this visit," Yonten would plead with Dawa, the only monk who was believed to have attained an accomplished level of meditation at Nala Monastery, "I could go to Chenrezig Pure Land a happy man."

Dawa would tell Yonten that his request would be considered—alongside that of many other requests received from his neighbors along the valley.

But Yonten was never chosen.

On the few occasions that Yonten came up in conversation at the monastery, the monks would mimic his request, always uttered in exactly the same words: "If you would kindly permit me to join you on this visit, I could go to Chenrezig Pure Land a happy man."

Kalsang would shake his head and say, "Poor, old Yonten. Fancy saying that. He can't even read!"

Dawa would say with a sigh, "Strange toothless fellow. I don't think he knows the first thing about how to meditate!"

One particular year, word got out that the Dalai Lama would be passing through Hemis imminently on his way to visit a gravely ill lama who was also a dear friend. Even though there was no planned teaching or blessing ceremony, this visit nevertheless presented an opportunity to catch a glimpse of His Holiness as he made his way along the road.

As in the past, Yonten presented himself at Nala monastery door, performed three full-length prostrations to both Kalsang and Dawa, individually, and beseeched them to let him join the traveling party.

As usual, both monks told him that his request would be considered, etcetera, etcetera.

As usual they didn't have the slightest intention of letting him come.

But something happened to change things. The pregnant wife of one of the pilgrims gave birth unexpectedly early. This meant that her husband, father and father-in-law all decided to stay behind. As did her mother and sister. Although the monks quickly allocated four of the five newly available places, they were still left with one place to fill.

There was no great enthusiasm to invite Yonten, and have to put up with his caved-in face and rheumy eyes and habit of noisily mashing his gums at erratic intervals, a routine as displeasing to the ear as his countenance was to the eye.

But the fact of the matter was that an extra back was needed to help carry the food the party would be eating on its out-bound journey, and bring back supplies of texts and other items the monks typically couriered home from Hemis. Yonten might be old, but he was also wiry, with the stamina of a mountain goat.

It was also true that the local monks weren't so completely unfeeling they didn't recognize how much the visit would mean to the old fellow. Feeling the very epitome of munificence, they summoned him to the monastery, told him that he could join the group, and watched him break down in tears of silent joy.

Giving him some time to regain his composure, Kalsang asked, "Have you ever seen a picture of His Holiness?"

"I think once. When I was a child," he replied. Before saying after a pause. "That may have been the thirteenth Dalai Lama."

Kalsang had reached into a drawer and taken out a head and shoulders photograph of His Holiness. "You may keep this as a gift," he said.

Receiving the photograph in both hands, Yonten stared at the image with the most profound devotion. "Today I have received the Buddha's blessings," said he.

Two days later, before daybreak, Yonten presented himself at the monastery and was loaded up like a pack horse. The canvas rucksack on his back was weighed down with so many metal food bowls and thermoses of butter tea, that he almost fell backwards. It was amazing he could stay upright, let alone move. But he was uncomplaining, and if he wondered why it was that several of the younger and more robust monks were far less encumbered, it was a thought that he kept to himself. All the way along the mountains, his silhouette was like a tortoise walking upright, somehow still able to whirl a prayer wheel, as he continued his practice of murmuring mantras wherever he went.

The party of twenty set off at the brisk pace required to get to Hemis before nightfall. There were occasional stops near mountain springs where they could drink fresh water. The only lengthier break was in the middle of the day when they stopped for lunch.

Relieved of his backpack, Yonten sat on the margins of the group, picking at the frugal meal he had brought to eat for the journey—a boiled potato, cheese and chili. For drink, he made do with water from a nearby stream.

The monks and villagers, meantime, feasted on the food he had helped carry on his back. The monastery kitchen and local families had gone to great lengths to ensure there was plenty of delicious food to nourish the pilgrims on their long journey. Sprawled on the grass, under the shade of a tree, they lounged beside plates loaded with tempting morsels, and took long draughts of butter tea.

While this was happening, one of the locals asked Venerable Kalsang if nirvana, the state of liberation was, like samsara, a physical place. This prompted the monk to offer the following explanation.

"Samsara and nirvana are not physical places. They are states of mind. We may think that we live in samsara, because we experience dissatisfaction. But the dissatisfaction isn't coming from the harshness of living in the mountains, or enduring the winter storms; it is coming from our minds when we perceive these things as causes of suffering. Someone else may experience the same phenomena that we do, but to them they are causes of delight.

"Take this butter tea." He held up his own mug. "To us, it is a nice, refreshing drink. To Westerners, it is a foul, disgusting liquid. To a hungry ghost it would be like pus. To a being from the deva realms, it is like nectar. What does that tell us?"

"That Westerners are like hungry ghosts?" offered one of the party.

They all had a good laugh before Kalsang shook his head. "What it tells us is that all comes from mind. Samsara or nirvana comes from mind. Whether a being is seen as ordinary or a Buddha tells us more about the mind of the perceiver than what is being perceived."

While the travelers discussed this subject amongst themselves, Yonten, who had been listening from a distance, nodded in agreement, smiling at the truth of what Kalsang had said and the clarity with which he had said it.

Looking over at him, it was only when a young boy, Tashi, suggested that the pilgrims might share some of their hearty meal and butter tea with their fellow traveler, that they agreed, spooning some of their leftovers onto a plate, which Tashi took over to the old man.

Yonten consumed the food and drink offered him with noisy appreciation, his table manners every bit as appalling as his fellow travelers had imagined they would be.

When they finally made it to Hemis that night, Dawa showed Yonten to his quarters: the corner of a storage shed round the back of the monastery washing block. The room had no door or window. Dawa handed Yonten two yak skins for a mattress.

It wasn't until the middle of the next day that the convoy of cars including His Holiness's approached Hemis Monastery. There was a wave of excitement as, first, a cloud of dust was seen in the distance, followed by the appearance of several four-wheel drive vehicles. The monks from Hemis surged to line the road, as did people from nearby mountains and valleys, all of them holding white scarves, or katags, as was the custom when preparing to meet eminent lamas.

The group from Nala valley was among them. Being an outsider, and someone who didn't push himself forward, Yonten didn't secure a spot directly at the roadside. Instead, he had to make do standing in the second row, doing his best to catch a glimpse of the Dalai Lama from between the heads of his fellow countrymen.

The Dalai Lama, wishing to be as available to as many people as possible, sat alone in the center back seat of one of the vehicles, with both windows down. Reaching the group of well-wishers, his vehicle reduced speed to slower than walking pace, His Holiness waved and brought his palms together at his heart as he looked from one side to the other, with his famous, beatific smile.

As always, wherever the Dalai Lama goes, the people who flocked to see him were moved in a way for which there are no words. It was as if His Holiness was able not only to see their own Buddha nature, but was somehow also able to reflect back the love and compassion they felt in their hearts. As always there was the knowledge that something special had happened, that they had encountered not only a holy being but one who had revealed to them their own highest nature.

After his convoy had gone by, there was a mood of euphoria and awe, of lightness and wellbeing. Monks and villagers turned to one another in laughter and joy.

No one paid much attention to Yonten, except for Tashi who saw him standing by himself with moist eyes and a rapturous smile.

"He is amazing, don't you think?!" exclaimed Tashi in his piping voice.

Yonten shook his head from side to side as though scarcely able to believe what he had just witnessed. "I never realized that the Dalai Lama had four arms," he said.

Tashi thought this a strange thing to say. His Holiness had two arms—he had seen that for himself. And seeing is believing.

Perhaps the old man was going senile?

Because it was too late to set off home, the pilgrims from Nala were to stay another night at Hemis Monastery. On their way back there, Tashi was walking alongside Kalsang, when he mentioned what Yonten had said to him. Kalsang had given him a very strange look.

"Are you quite sure he said that?" he asked.

"Of course."

"You're not making up stories?"

"Why would I?"

Squeezing his shoulder, Kalsang took a few steps away from the path, where he could scan the whole group, before spotting Yonten, and making his way towards him.

As Kalsang was well aware, Chenrezig, the Buddha of Compassion, had four arms symbolizing love, compassion, joy and equanimity. If Yonten had seen the Dalai Lama, said to be a living manifestation of Chenrezig, in his purest form, that would make him a practitioner of supreme accomplishment. Certainly more accomplished than any of the monks at Nala Monastery—quite probably any of those at Hemis too!

"So, Yonten—" he approached the old man "—was it good to see His Holiness?"

Yonten was still shaking his head. "I never realized that the Dalai Lama had four arms," he repeated the same words.

"You saw them yourself?"

"Didn't everyone?"

"We all saw His Holiness," replied Kalsang, beginning to recognize just how greatly he and his fellow monks had misjudged the toothless old peasant. And starting to regret, very deeply, their treatment of him.

Remembering how they'd loaded him up like a mule the day before, Kalsang said, "I am sorry we made you carry so much on your back when we came here yesterday."

"Were you not offering the gift of purification?" asked Yonten.

Kalsang remained silent as they continued on the path back to Hemis. When he spoke again he said, "I'm also sorry we didn't share more of our picnic and butter tea."

"Oh!" Yonten seemed surprised. "I remember being presented with only the most delightful foods and nectars. More than I could possibly eat."

Finally, they reached the storage shed, round the back of the monastery washing block, where Yonten had slept the night before. Kalsang glanced around at the unprepossessing austerity—not so much as a window or even a door, and the feeling of being cast out from where everyone else was staying.

"And I'm sorry they made you sleep here last night. I'll see to it that you are moved."

"But this is a wonderful place!" enthused Yonten. "I thought you had reserved the best spot for me! This is my celestial mansion. Now I can go to Chenrezig Pure Land a happy man."

So adamant was Yonten that Kalsang didn't push things further. Except to say, "I will come and fetch you when our evening meal is served."

Returning to the Nala monks, Kalsang told them everything that Yonten had said, before concluding:

"I think the old man was being sincere in his speech. Which means he perceives the purest nature of everything around him."

"But how can an illiterate peasant do that?" asked one of the men. "What does he know of the Dharma?"

"He is not even a monk," objected another. "He has taken no vows or precepts."

"What does he understand about meditation?" asked someone else. "Is he even aware of how to train the mind?"

After much discussion, the nine monks decided they should all go to visit Yonten before supper. That would give them all the chance to question him first hand and listen carefully to his answers.

At twilight, the Nala monks made their way to the shed around the back of the monastery. The sun was setting and the sky was cloudless so that, from one horizon to the other, the sky was a sweep of boundless radiance and clarity, the purity of the mountain light revealing all with a pristine timelessness.

Their footsteps slowing as they approached the shed, a short distance before reaching the open doorway, the small group paused. Taking the lead, Kalsang walked the few remaining steps to the door, stopping just before he reached it.

"Yonten! We are here to collect you!" he called out.

There was no response.

"Louder!" urged one of the monks behind him.

Kalsang repeated his greeting in a more commanding voice.

To be met, once again, only with silence.

Stepping closer, Kalsang looked through the open door. The corner of the shed, where the yak skins had been placed, seemed empty at first. He glanced all around, and upwards, to check there wasn't some other place in the shed where the old man might be waiting. But there wasn't.

"He must have gone somewhere," Kalsang announced, half turning to the group.

As he did so, something caught his eye. On the yak skin were several items of clothing he recognized as belonging to Yonten. And as he looked closer, he could also see the prayer wheel from which Yonten was never separated.

"Wait!" he said, his voice conveying a rare urgency and importance.

The others joined him as he stepped into the shed, took a few steps to the yak skins, and bent over in inspection.

There could be no doubting it. These were the clothes Yonten had been wearing earlier that day. The shoes, pants and jacket. The prayer wheel he held at all times, *and* the mala—or rosary beads—he kept wound about his wrist. And were those his finger-nails scattered on the floor too?

"He said he would go to the pure land of Chenrezig a happy man." It was Dawa, the yogi, who voiced what they all were thinking.

Kalsang brought his palms together at his heart in an act of spontaneous prostration. "It seems like he has done exactly that."

That evening, the atmosphere in the dining hall at Hemis monastery was one of a heady exhilaration sensed by every single person in the room. The festive atmosphere that had accompanied His Holiness's rare appearance that day had been followed by the electrifying news of what had happened to Yonten. Word of his miraculous dissolution had spread through the corridors and temples, the bedrooms and courtyards in an instant. Nothing so exciting had happened at Hemis monastery—frankly, any monastery in the Himalayas—for years!

The ability of a practitioner to dissolve his gross, physical body into clear light was so rare as to be virtually unheard of. When it had happened in the past, the practitioner had already been a known yogi or highly experienced meditation practitioner. Yonten didn't fit that description. In fact, he had shown no sign of possessing any special attainments at all. Yet it seemed that, within the past few hours, he had transferred his consciousness to a very different realm of experience—his goal since the days of Lama Palden.

While it wasn't customary for the Abbot of Hemis to address monks in the dining hall after they had eaten, there was nothing customary about what was happening today. And, given all the questions and confusion, the feverish speculation and theories about Yonten, which were already beginning to multiply rapidly, the abbot decided now was a time to offer an explanation.

After acknowledging the extraordinary events of the day, and the excitement felt by each one of them—resident monks as well as their visitors—he made his way quickly to the question that lay at the heart of all their conversations that evening.

"How was it possible?" he asked. The abbot, a stockily-built and jovial monk, well-known for his encyclopedic knowledge of the sutras, tantras and commentaries, was also well informed about what was being said in the passages of his own monastery.

"Our tradition places special emphasis on wisdom. Wisdom goes further than mere knowledge. It requires a practitioner to understand and embody that knowledge in their every action of body, speech and mind. Many people are saying today, 'How could

Yonten make this extraordinary transition, when he couldn't even read or write?'

"Our teachings also place great emphasis on meditation practice. Without it, how can we begin to understand the true nature of mind? How can we perceive our own gross consciousness, much less experience the nature of our most subtle states of mind? Again, people are saying, "Yonten had no training in any of this. He was a simple man, a peasant farmer. Whatever meditation he may have done was without the benefit of any formal instruction."

"What has happened at Hemis today is truly extraordinary. Perhaps a once-in-a-lifetime event. What Yonten has just done is amazing!" His words rang out. "Remarkable!" Then lowering his voice for dramatic emphasis, he said, "We should all rejoice in what Yonten achieved—and what we can learn from him."

The abbot allowed time for his words to sink in, before continuing. "Yonten's spiritual attainment was made possible because of one thing—his faith: faith not in a belief, or a wish or a dream, but in a process. Instead of 'faith' I prefer to call this quality 'conviction'.

"Yonten had complete conviction in the practice shown him by his teacher, Lama Palden. And why should he not? It is a practice that has led millions of beings to enlightenment since the time of the Buddha. A practice available to us all. Yonten recited the sacred mantra of Chenrezig ceaselessly. He did so for decades repeating the mantra while turning his prayer wheel. In doing this, he engaged his body, speech and mind in a process that drew him closer and closer to Chenrezig.

"It didn't matter that he couldn't read—step by step his thoughts were purified by his practice until his whole experience of reality was one of transcendental bliss. He may not have been sitting on a meditation cushion, but what is the Buddhist definition of meditation? 'The thorough familiarization of the mind with virtue.' Was this not what Yonten was doing as he walked the mountains, reciting mantras?

"So you see, spiritual attainment does not necessarily depend on great learning or even meditative accomplishment. Whatever our Dharma practice, if we are diligent, with a good heart and strong conviction, we too can be like Yonten.

"Enlightenment is not just for accomplished yogis, or learned monks and nuns. Yonten may have been a simple man, but remember the words of the famous masters Geshe Chengawa and Geshe Acharya Thubten Loden: 'In the summer observe which becomes greener, the high tops of the mountain or the moist valleys resting below! It is the humble mind that flourishes in the Dharma.'"

Next day, the group from Nala valley, monks and lay people, set off home.

There had been some discussion about what to do with Yonten's clothes, prayer wheel and fingernails—now considered to be the relics of a holy man. The Nala monks had suggested the relics be left at Hemis Monastery, where Yonten had dissolved into clear light. But the abbot of Hemis instructed them differently. "Take them home and build a stupa, as a constant inspiration to the people of Nala," said he.

When asked where, exactly, the stupa should be built, he had told them, somewhat mysteriously, that the location would become obvious.

Trekking back across the mountains, the small band of pilgrims was still at least an hour away from home when they encountered a small group of fellow countrymen from the Nala Valley. The group began waving and calling out to them, as soon as they came into view.

Pretty soon they were joined by others from along the valley. All were in a similar state of excitement. All urged them to hurry back home as quickly as possible, to witness the most curious phenomenon.

Ever since the afternoon before, they told the returning pilgrims, the boulder where Yonten often used to sit had been shrouded in rainbow-colored lights.

The Nala pilgrims in turn shared their own story of what had happened at Hemis Monastery. At which point everything made special and wonderful sense!

The fatigue of the pilgrims, after a full day's hike, was no barrier in their wish to return home to witness the rainbow lights for themselves. They strode as fast as their legs would carry them along the mountains, gathering more and more farmers along the way.

As the story of Yonten was told and re-told, and they recognized they were all witnesses to the most extraordinary spiritual attainment, their excitement grew.

Until they reached the place of Yonten's boulder.

Sure enough, it was still bathed in the most dazzling array of rainbow lights, which emanated and returned into the great rock, seeming to transform the stone itself into the nature of rainbow-colored light.

As Yonten's fellow neighbors from Nala valley and the nearby monastery approached the boulder, something of the transcendent bliss that pervaded the place touched their hearts.

"We made a great error disrespecting Yonten and not being his friend because he couldn't read or write," Kalsang was the first to confess.

"And because he couldn't meditate," said Dawa.

"And because he was so ugly," chimed a neighbor.

"But none of these is an obstacle to enlightenment," said Kalsang.

"Or to acquainting the mind with virtue," agreed Dawa.

"Or to manifesting a beautiful rainbow body," offered the neighbor.

At this moment, unable to resist the enchantment any longer, young Tashi ran across to the boulder and was caught up in the rainbow lights, dancing and laughing as he felt them ripple through his whole body.

"We build his stupa here?" he asked, jumping up and down on the spot where Yonten used to sit, watching his small herd of yaks and goats.

"A testament to the power of mantra," agreed Kalsang.

If you travel to the Nala Valley in Ladakh today, and ask the local farmers, you, too, can find your way to Yonten's stupa at the foot of the great, slanting boulder. It is a modest, whitewashed structure that stands beside that very large rock. A memorial to the toothless old peasant who, through the power of mantra, so cultivated his mind that when he looked at the Dalai Lama, he saw not a monk, but the Buddha of Compassion himself. A reminder that sometimes behind the most forbidding of faces abides the purest of hearts.

THE SERA STREET BOOK CLUB

IF WE ARE VERY LUCKY, IT HAPPENS ONCE OR TWICE IN OUR LIFE: A BOOK comes into our hands with exactly the right message at the very moment we need to hear it most of all. A message that helps us find the courage to make the changes we need if we are to flourish. An insight that helps us let go of a way of being that no longer serves us well. A revelation that opens our eyes to a different reality we never even guessed at, but that was right there all along in the people and places around us, the connections we feel in our hearts.

That morning, scanning the Biography shelves at *Bound to Please*, Jenny had no idea that anything unusual was about to happen—that she was about to set in motion events which would change her own life and the lives of three very dear friends in the most extraordinary way.

What she did know was that it was her turn to choose the next book club title. And she was struggling. She had already spent over half an hour going through the Latest Releases shelves as well as the

Bestsellers. Now onto non-fiction, her eyes paused for a moment on the cover of *The Life and Wisdom of Lama Lotsawa*.

She had never heard of this particular lama. The picture was of a monk with a kindly but unfamiliar face. Only because she was getting desperate, she picked it up.

According to the back cover, Lama Lotsawa had been a Tibetan monk driven from his country into exile in 1959. Having reached the safety of India, he had created a sanctuary to help take care of young monks and nuns, many still only children, who had also been pursued through the treacherous mountain passes of the Himalayas by the Red Army.

Some of the best-known lamas in the West had, at one time, been cared for by Lama Lotsawa. As Jenny flicked through the pages, she saw the book contained stories as well as teachings. There were poignant black and white photographs of those early days in India, including youthful versions of lamas who had become well known in the West. On impulse, she decided to get the book for the club. She grabbed the four remaining copies from the shelf.

The book would do, she reckoned, for their next meeting. The title of the month was no longer such an important subject of discussion as it had been in the past. The Sera Street Book Club had become a lot less bookish and a lot more social of late.

They had been going for nearly 20 years, their number rising and falling through the marriages, pregnancies and divorces of various members. At the peak, three or so years ago, there had been eight regulars. All the while, the same four women who had established it had remained as its core. And just as the passage of time hardly seemed to change the way they thought about each other, it had also left, undiminished, their sense of wonder that they had always got on so well, even though they had absolutely nothing in common apart from the club. And their age: 58 and counting.

Inez, a violinist who played in the orchestra, was slender, dark haired and tempestuous—something the others put down to her Italian genes. The ever-disheveled Fi was a language academic at the local university, never failing to pick up at least one or two copy errors in any book that they read, and sometimes surprisingly more. They used to tease Michelle for being a lady who lunched, being the wife of a successful garden furniture manufacturer, her blonde hair, make-up and clothing always immaculate. Jenny herself was the only club member who was single, her husband Craig having died of a heart attack five years earlier. A matronly woman with a kindly face, she had been left well-off enough by Craig's life insurance policy that she was able to spend several days each week at a nearby hospice, working as a voluntary palliative care visitor— usually accompanied by her much-loved golden retriever, Barry.

"Something Tibetan again!" Fi had put on her glasses to inspect her copy of *The Life and Wisdom of Lama Lotsawa* at the club meeting the following week. "It's been a while."

"A bit different from all the murder mysteries," observed Michelle.

"Remember how serious we were in the early days?" Inez got up from Jenny's dining room table to splash generous helpings of Tempranillo into each of their glasses.

"'The Spiritual Seekers Book Club'." Jenny reminded them of the name they had originally planned for themselves, before deciding it sounded too pretentious. In those far off, early days, almost all their book choices had been from the Mind Body Spirit or Tibetan Buddhism shelves of their local bookstores. "We used to meditate at the start of our meetings."

"I miss that!" sighed Inez.

"We were going to keep a written review of every book we read, remember Fi?" said Jenny turning to Fi. They all thought of Fi as the organized one when it came to documenting responses to what they read. "We thought we'd become so very wise if we read one book a month for years and years."

"Twenty years later," chimed Michelle. "I don't feel very much wiser."

"I don't think we've even got a list of all the books we've read," noted Fi. "Thank heavens for Jenny's "system"."

They glanced at the wall in Jenny's sitting room where Craig had installed floor-to-ceiling bookshelves. Jenny's "system" was, quite simply, to place each book they finished next to the previous one. The result was over 200 books reaching from their most recent, all the way back to their very first: *The Art of Happiness*.

"I suppose as other people joined us, we broadened out a bit," observed Michelle.

"In more ways than one." Fi stroked her stomach ruefully as they all chuckled. For many of the previous months, years even, they had been working their way through mystery and chick lit novels, with a few periods of more literary choices mixed in.

"But it's been just us, these past couple of months," observed Inez. "The good old gang of four."

Raising their wine glasses, they chimed them together. "Through thick and thin," they chanted gleefully, as they often did when it was just them.

"Though how we came together," Inez said, repeating the oft-made observation, "I simply do not know!"

Their routine, on monthly book club evenings, was for Michelle to collect Fi, who lived in the neighboring suburb. On the way to book club they'd stop at Kathmandu, a Nepalese takeaway for their standard order. Fi would go in for the food and an obligatory hug from Mrs. Tenzin, who spoke no English but adored her, and who always insisted they take a small bag of prawn crackers, free of charge, for Barry, who she always called Dorje for some inscrutable reason. Then they'd make the short drive to Jenny's.

Inez, who had family connections in the wine business, would arrive with reds or whites, depending on whatever she was able to lay her hands on. Jenny provided coffee, dessert and the venue.

They had started by rotating around each other's houses, but had gravitated to Jenny's home in Sera Street because it somehow *felt* right. The home was very Jenny, with light catchers in the windows, Balinese wind chimes in the trees outside and a large, blue Buddha portrait on the dining room wall, watching over them. The other group members thought of Jenny as being a bit fey—if anything paranormal was going to happen, Fi would jokingly complain, it always seemed to happen to Jenny.

It was a complaint that they would soon never make again.

Four weeks later, the night before the next book club meeting, Michelle was on the sofa at home with *The Life and Wisdom of Lama Lotsawa.*

"What's it this month?" her husband Glenn asked, glancing up from where he was browsing through European furniture catalogs beside her.

She showed him the cover.

"Any good?"

"I've only just started."

"Last-minute cramming?" He delivered a mock-censorious expression.

"I know." She shrugged. "But just look at this."

While flicking through the book, which, frankly, was as far as she'd got, she had paused at one of the sets of black and white photographs. One photograph, in particular, had caught her attention. It showed three novice monks and a dog. Two of the novices looked about 11 or 12 and their camera smiles couldn't disguise their earnest expressions. The third looked about eight. In his left hand he was holding a piece of twine, attached to the collar of the dog. His right was resting on the dog's head, who he was regarding with affection.

"Tibetan terrier," observed Glenn.

"How do you know that?" She was surprised.

"Distinctive look," he told her. "And they're not really terriers. The Europeans who named them were mistaken."

It was one of the many times when Michelle was surprised by her husband's general knowledge. But it wasn't the dog, specifically, that gave her pause. There seemed something so vulnerable about the small group of them standing in their robes and sandals, the little one loving his pet dog. Beneath the photograph, the caption read: "A group of novice monks about to flee from Lhasa in 1959." In sandals, and with a dog, observed Michelle. Did they even stand a chance?

In the next-door suburb, Fi was similarly engaged in last-minute study as she sat at the dining table after supper. Just like Michelle, she was similarly struck by the same black and white photograph of the three monks.

"Look at these three," she remarked as her partner, Mike, made his way to the kitchen to make coffee.

He scanned the date. "1959. They don't look equipped for any kind of journey. You wonder if they ever made it."

The vulnerability of the trio with their pet dog was almost palpable. Which was why, thought Fi, the picture had been chosen for the book. But there was something else about that photograph that held her attention. An inexplicable sense of connection.

Inez had felt the same thing too. Even though an advertisement sound track had swallowed up a lot of her time since their last meeting, that same photograph of the three novice monks haunted her too.

As for Jenny, she had felt powerfully tugged to the image of the three novices, staring at it until almost moved to tears.

In the early hours of the night before the next book club meeting, shortly before dawn, the girls had a dream. The same, lucid dream. And what's more, they knew that each of the others were having it, because they were all in it together sharing what happened as clearly as everyday reality.

They were sitting around the dining table at Jenny's house, in their familiar places, when a Tibetan lama appeared from the hallway. The lama wasn't some ghostly apparition, but appeared as much flesh and blood as they were. Sixty something, in monk's robes, as soon as he arrived, the girls intuitively knew him as the lama from the book.

He didn't appear exactly like the monk whose photograph was on the front cover. He was somehow a younger version. He carried himself with a straight back and was a commanding presence. As he turned to look at them, there was something else in his eyes to which they instantly responded: it was, quite simply, the most compassionate acceptance that they had ever experienced. They felt as though he knew them, through and through. As he made eye contact with each one of them, bowing towards them, he seemed to recognize all that was most loving and pure in their hearts, and reflect it back to them so that, in that moment, they caught a glimpse of their own true nature. The radiant love and peace of the experience made them melt.

When he turned away, the girls exchanged wide-eyed glances. A human-size hourglass had appeared in the center of the room, the larger volume of golden sand in the glass sphere at the top streaming steadily into the bottom, turning ash colored as it did so. Lama

Lotsawa walked towards Craig's shelves and placed the index finger of his right hand on the spine of *The Art of Happiness*, their very first book choice, before running his finger along the shelf, across each of the book club titles. His finger continued to move steadily some way before pausing on a mystery story. Touching it with his fingertip, the book immediately spun off the shelf in an arc towards the floor behind him. Before reaching the floor, it had dissolved, vanished, leaving behind only an empty spot on the shelf.

On the top shelf he tapped very few books. But as he reached the second shelf, there were more and more deletions. The girls couldn't see exactly which books he was dismissing. They didn't need to. One way or another, they knew that the books he touched had nothing to do with the original purpose of their group. They had not, in any meaningful way, contributed to their spiritual development.

As the monk continued, he reached shelves where he tapped almost every book. Book after book spun into nothingness, leaving great gaps behind. And in that curious way of dreams, time took on the strangest dimension so that only a minute of ordinary time was needed to feel like the passage of twenty years.

In the hourglass, there was now far more sand in the lower sphere than the upper one, and what remained in the upper one was rapidly flowing out. Lama Lotsawa was beginning to stoop, the color draining from his skin as he became elderly and frail. Running his finger along the final titles, he was tapping every book, leaving whole shelves vacant. Except for the very last one, *The Life and Wisdom of Lama Lotsawa*. As he looked at it, it flew to the dining table, turning into four copies and landing at an open page in front of each one of them.

Now a wizened old man, he turned, looking directly at them with a sadness that was unbearable. His eyes meeting theirs again, each of the women felt his grief with the same level of intensity that they had previously felt his love and acceptance. It was a heartbreaking, acutely-felt sense of lost opportunity. Of a precious life that could never be re-lived. Of terrible waste.

The books that remained behind him had turned into pure gold, but instead of shelves and shelves filled with gold, there were relatively few, glowing volumes, and many empty spaces between.

The remaining sand in the hourglass had almost completely drained. The lama turned to leave. As he did, he decayed completely, turning into a skeleton before their eyes and walking into the hourglass—both of them collapsing into dust before this, too, vanished.

The girls turned to each other, shaken.

What they saw troubled them even more. Each one of them had become very old women, with sunken cheeks, white hair and cadaverous bodies.

"I can't believe this is happening!" wailed Fi.

"We've got to *do* something!" Inez was passionate.

They looked down at the copy of the book, open at the particular chapter. It was entitled "Impermanence and death'.

"Tomorrow we will discuss this chapter." Jenny was firm.

Next day, all four of them studied the chapter with unprecedented zeal. Michelle read it first thing in the morning. Fi closed the door to her office at work, telling colleagues she was undertaking an urgent literature review. Inez skipped a chamber group rehearsal to make time. Jenny, who had already read the chapter, re-read it.

They had, of course, exchanged texts and messages about the dream as soon as they'd woken. Not that they'd needed to. They already knew it had been a shared experience—the most powerful of their lives!

They got ready for their next meeting with greater anticipation than ever before. Michelle was at Fi's place five minutes ahead of schedule. When Fi appeared, she got out the car and the two of them embraced—not something they usually did. But there nothing usual about what was happening.

They got to Kathmandu a few minutes before their meal was ready. Instead of waiting in the car while Fi went in for the food, Michelle joined her so the two of them could keep talking. As Fi paid for their meal at the counter, next to her Michelle glanced over the community noticeboard, spotting a stack of fliers for a visiting lama who would be coming to town in a couple of week's time.

She was showing the flier to Fi when Mrs. Tenzin emerged from behind the scenes, and made a great fuss, hugging them both. When she saw the brochure Michelle was holding she became very excited, and kept touching her heart—they gathered that the lama, Doringpa Rinpoche, was her own teacher. They left a few minutes later with their meal plus free prawn crackers—and a copy of the flier.

"What was *that* all about?" Michelle asked when they were all seated round Jenny's dining room table, food on their plates and wine poured.

Eyes shining after their extraordinary experience, they had never felt such closeness. Or anticipation.

"Did anyone else think he was ..." began Inez.

"Lama Lotsawa?" suggested Jenny.

"Nothing like the cover pic," observed Fi. "But I just *knew* it was him."

From the way the others were nodding, it was evident they had known too.

"What I've been thinking today," said Michelle, "is why? Why Lama Lotsawa? Why last night? Why didn't we have the same dream years ago when reading some of those Buddhist books?"

Fi was blunt. "Maybe we didn't need the kick up the bum that we do now."

"Perhaps we have a connection to him that we haven't had to others," suggested Jenny.

The others looked at her closely.

"This is going to sound really bad," Fi confessed. "But I hadn't read any of the book before going to sleep last night. I'd only flicked through the photos."

"I thought it was just me." Michelle stared at the table before sneaking a glance at Fi. "Last night after supper I had the best of intentions. Last-minute cramming, as Glenn puts it. But I ended up just going through the photos. One in particular—"

"The three monks!" the others chorused, exchanging a meaningful expression.

It was a while before Jenny said, "I just felt a shiver run down my spine."

From the looks on the others' faces, it was clear they'd had the same experience.

"So—" Jenny was trying to remain calm through the continuing revelations "—we were all … strongly affected by the photograph?"

"I pointed it out to Glenn," said Michelle.

"I did to Mike." Fi tilted her head in the direction of her home.

"The pathos!" Tears welled in Inez's eyes as she summed up their feelings about the three boys and their pet dog.

By contrast, on the floor beside them, Barry the golden retriever had long since vacuumed up the last of his prawn crackers.

"And … from that image," persisted Jenny "came the dream?"

"And the message in the dream," said Fi.

"D'you think Lama Lotsawa's still alive?" Michelle turned to Fi, the font on all matters authorial.

"I was wondering exactly the same thing," chimed Fi.

"It doesn't say anything in the book about him dying." Inez touched her copy.

"The book was published seven years ago," said Fi. "He was a very old man, even then. I did some online searches today, but didn't come up with anything. I wanted to find out if he's still here. And what connection we might possibly have to him."

There was a long pause before Jenny said, "His message was unmistakable."

The others murmured in agreement.

"The same, pretty much, as in that chapter," said Michelle.

The chapter they had all made exceptional efforts to read had quoted Lama Lotsawa's teachings on impermanence and death. How our usual, human tendency is to shun all thought of our own mortality.

To imagine that our death is perpetually somewhere over the horizon. Even when shaken by the death of a loved one, or a brush with a dread disease, after a period of time we revert to our usual complacency.

Lama Lotsawa pointed out that this avoidance is nothing short of tragic. That there was good reason why Buddha had always said that imagining our own death was the greatest meditation of all. Because when we don't flinch from contemplating the reality that death is certain, and the time of it uncertain, when we try to imagine, as vividly as possible, the truth that we could die right now, today—*that* is when we awaken to the true value of life. We realize just how finite and precious it is. And recognizing our fragile hold on this tenuous and ever-changing experience, we are encouraged to make the most of it. To prioritize what is important. To focus on the people and pursuits that are meaningful, and not to waste time doing things simply out of habit, or to meet the expectations of others.

The girls discussed the chapter over dinner—how hard it had been to read. How much it had challenged their views. They referred to some of the other books they had read, back in the early days.

It was Jenny who summed up their feelings. "More than anything else," she said, toying with the stem of her wine glass, "what's happened has been the biggest wake up call."

The others murmured their agreement.

"Remember how, last meeting, you said that we'd been so serious, back in the early days?" Fi turned to Inez. "After the dream, you can't help thinking how much more useful it would have been if we *had* read hundreds of books by wise teachers, instead of all those murder mysteries and chick lit."

"At least we're not dead yet," responded Jenny.

"Not like at the end of the dream," said Michelle.

There was a collective shudder.

"That was the whole point, wasn't it?" offered Inez. "To get us back on track."

The others were nodding.

"So, we keep on reading *The Life and Wisdom of Lama Lotsawa*?" proposed Jenny.

"And I'm going to investigate the author and that photo," announced Fi. "See if I can find out more about the three monks."

Towards the end of the evening, they agreed on another thing too: they would attend the public talk given by the visiting lama, Doringpa Rinpoche, in two week's time. It was being held in a school hall only twenty minutes drive away. After everything else that had happened, it was an easy call to make.

Two weeks later, on the way to the talk, Fi brought them up to date with her investigations. All four of them were in Michelle's car as she headed north. Fi had tracked down an email address for the author of *The Life and Wisdom of Lama Lotsawa*. Explaining how much the book had meant to members of her book club, she asked about Lama Lotsawa—was he still alive and, if so, where did he live? She also said how one particular photograph had resonated very strongly with members of her book club. She wondered if he had any knowledge of the novice monks pictured, and whether they had escaped to freedom.

The author had replied within days. Yes, he said, Lama Lotsawa was still alive at the age of 91, a revered master at a monastery in Ladakh, India. And while he didn't know what had become of the boys, he said that he had included the photo in the book at the express instruction of Lama Lotsawa. The lama had hoped that, by getting the picture out into the world, some reconnection may be possible. Lama Lotsawa had himself wanted to know what had become of them—they had been his students back in old Tibet.

There were only around ten people when they arrived at the school hall. Fi led them to the last of several rows of chairs, but Inez countered her.

"You have no idea how disheartening it is to appear in front of an audience and they're all sitting far away from you," she lectured them. They meekly followed her to the very front row.

Other people trickled in as they got closer to 6 pm. There were no more than 30 or so when a door opened to the side of the room and in came a handful of Tibetan people including Mrs. Tenzin, who was dressed formally, and wore a large necklace studded with turquoise that gave her an almost regal appearance. They took reserved seats alongside the girls, before the speaker emerged.

When he did, it was as though a light had been switched on in the room. Doringpa Rinpoche had a glow about him, even a playfulness that caught them by surprise. They had come expecting piety and devotion, but holding his palms to his heart and bowing to the group as he scanned the audience, his eyes met theirs and he smiled with amusement, as though sharing a joke with people he already knew.

The girls exchanged glances.

A sense of lightness and joy pervaded his twenty-minute lecture on loving kindness. During it, early on, he mentioned that his own kind root guru was Lama Lotsawa.

The girls had the hardest time paying attention to that evening's talk after that, with so many thoughts coming into their heads. Thoughts like: what is going on with these freakish connections? The way they were all drawn to the same photograph in the book. How they'd all been involved in the same lucid dream. How they'd just happened to have found a flier for tonight's talk at their local restaurant—for a teacher who also just happened to be the student of Lama Lotsawa.

At the end of the talk, the girls held back while a few other members of the audience went to speak to their visitor briefly. Then they approached him together.

After they had exchanged greetings and thanks, Fi held up a copy of *The Life and Wisdom of Lama Lotsawa*. "We've been studying this book," she said.

"Very good." He nodded in recognition—and that playful and even somewhat mischievous glint was in his eye as he glanced from one to the other of them.

"We were all strongly affected when we saw this photograph." She turned to the page, and held it out for him to inspect.

He glanced towards it. "Yes, yes."

"We were thinking, seeing that your teacher is Lama Lotsawa, perhaps you can tell us something about these boys."

"In Tibet I knew them very well." He nodded. "That was many years ago."

"You knew them?!" Inez was animated.

"We lived in the same village," said Rinpoche. "The older two boys were my cousins. Family."

Mrs. Tenzin approached the group and interjected, saying something to the lama in Tibetan. He appeared to agree with what she suggested.

"We go for supper to her restaurant. Yes?"

They were shown to a table in the covered veranda at the back. The girls were surprised to find it was just them and Doringpa Rinpoche sitting around a table. Others who had attended the talk, including the Tibetans, were sitting at a different table a short distance away, while Mrs. Tenzin liaised with the kitchen.

It was Michelle, always the most outspoken of the four, who wanted to get things out in the open.

"A couple of weeks ago we had the same dream, all four of us, when we thought we saw Lama Lotsawa. We had this feeling that the dream was somehow triggered by the photograph of the three boys."

Reaching out, for a few moments Rinpoche took the hands of Jenny and Fiona who sat to either side of him.

"You really want to know about the boys?" he asked.

"Their clothes, in that photograph!" exclaimed Inez. "They couldn't walk through the Himalayas in robes and sandals."

"And the little dog," said Jenny. "It broke my heart thinking about what could have happened."

"Since nineteen fifty-one, the Chinese were trying to take over Tibet," Rinpoche began, his expression earnest. "The Red Army had already occupied some parts of the country. When soldiers began to move towards Lhasa, the capital, it didn't take us all by surprise. For the boys and for me, our home was Sera."

"Sera?" asked Jenny.

"Sera Monastery. One of the three great Gelug monasteries."

"My home is in Sera," Jenny glanced about the table. "Sera Street."

Rinpoche looked unsurprised by this apparent coincidence. "We were all young enough," he continued, "that when we had to flee we also had a sense of adventure. We looked forward to going somewhere new. We had all these ideas about the wonderful world we'd find on the other side of the mountains."

He looked at Jenny. "You'll be pleased to know that they didn't take Dorje, the dog, with them. He stayed with a family in the village and had a long, happy life."

They smiled.

Expression turning sombre, he met Inez's gaze. "But you are right about the boys. Their clothes were completely inadequate. They didn't have any food. They wouldn't have lasted a week in the mountains. But they never made it that far. The day after that photograph was taken, the first Red Army troops arrived in Lhasa. All four of them were shot dead."

The girls slumped back in their chairs. The connection each one of them had felt to the monks gave the news an impact that was inexplicably personal.

It was Michelle who was the first to recover sufficiently to say, "Four. You said four boys. But there were only three."

"Plus the one behind the camera. A boy called Jampa," he said.

Fi was looking confused. "If they were killed in 1959, surely Lama Lotsawa would have got to hear about it?"

"Of course." Doringpa Rinpoche nodded.

"The author of this book—" she took it out of her handbag, and opened it out for him at the appropriate page "—said he included the photograph at the lama's request because he wanted to know what became of them."

"He did," said the monk. "He does."

All four women were looking bewildered.

"And soon, I will be able to tell him."

Then as he glanced at their confused expressions. "Let me explain a little about these ones. Kalsang—" he gestured to one of the older boys "—my cousin. When he got to freedom he had set his heart on the amazing things he'd once seen in a film about the West. He especially liked the beautiful homes and cars." He smiled at Michelle. "Wonderful lifestyle."

"Palden—" he looked at Fi "—always had his nose in a text. He liked to study. He wanted to spend more time with books and learned people. Palden was also my cousin."

"This little one, Tinley, the village favorite, he liked to sing and dance. Very musical."

Inez put her hands to her heart as she stared at the poignant photo of the little child with the tattered clothing and affectionate expression, holding the leash made from string.

"The one behind the camera, Jampa ..." He gazed at Jenny. "He also wanted to be in the photograph, but the boys could borrow the camera only for one photo. It was very precious—film was so expensive. They couldn't all be in the photo and Jampa was always kind, self-sacrificing, thinking of others. So he offered to take the photograph and not be in it."

By now, the connections couldn't have been more self-evident. Tears filled their eyes as they wept silently, realizing the truth of their deep connections to the boys in the photograph, to each other, to Lama Lotsawa and to Rinpoche.

None of the events of the past few weeks had been coincidence! Only now were they beginning to recognize the powerful bonds to their previous life that had surrounded them their whole lives, and to which they had been so oblivious.

"Lama Lotsawa came to bring us back to the path," Jenny managed in a cracked voice.

Rinpoche squeezed her hand briefly. "Our kind root guru, Lama Lotsawa, has been waiting for many decades, wanting to hear from you directly. You know, there are many in the West, born around 1959 and in the years afterwards, who have a connection to Tibet, same as you." Then as he watched them dabbing at their tear-stained eyes, "But an enlightened being, no matter how powerful, can't just pop out of nowhere. Something needs to come from the side of the student. From your side. You needed to reach out."

"Like getting the book?" asked Fi.

"Yes."

"Well. We want to be back in touch," she confirmed.

"Having wasted so much time!" bemoaned Michelle.

"What is important is to make the most of opportunities here and now. You four—" he beamed at them all "—you have a very special connection."

"We always used to joke we had nothing in common!" Inez's mouth was twisted with emotion.

It was Rinpoche's turn to laugh. "You have *everything* in common! In particular, the Buddha, his teachings and your special fellow students. Buddha, Dharma and Sangha. You have felt the heart connection, yes?"

They were nodding as Mrs. Tenzin arrived back in the room with plates loaded with dumplings.

"This is my mother." Rinpoche put his arm around her waist.

"Mrs. Tenzin?!" Fi couldn't contain herself.

"Kalsang and Palden were her nephews," he continued. "Tinley and Jampa were good friends in the village. She knew each one of you in your last lifetime." He gestured them one by one, circling his finger.

As Fi exchanged a tearful smile with Rinpoche's mother, she couldn't help feeling bad about all the times she'd complained about what a fuss Mrs. Tenzin made over her.

"She is, what do you say in English, clairvoyant," said Rinpoche.

Fi hardly knew how to react. Which was when the old Tibetan lady came over to embrace her and Inez warmly.

She had known who they were even when they hadn't known it themselves. Which was why her pleasure in seeing them had always been so heartfelt.

"I must spend some time with the other guests." Rinpoche excused himself, getting up and moving to one of the other tables. Then smiling at Jenny, he said, "Give Dorje a pat from me."

"You mean my dog Barry is …?"

"Dorje. Come back. Better food in the West!" he chuckled, rubbing his tummy, before stepping away.

If we are very lucky, it happens once or twice in our life: a book comes into our hands with exactly the right message at the very moment we need to hear it most of all. A message that helps us find the courage to make the changes we need if we are to flourish. An insight that helps us let go of a way of being that no longer serves us well. A revelation that opens our eyes to a different reality we never even guessed at, but that was right there all along in the people and places around us, the connections we feel in our hearts.

THE ASTRAL TRAVELER'S HANDBOOK

ONCE UPON A TIME THERE WAS A VERY NICE, YOUNG MAN WHO HAD an unusual ambition. At 25 years of age, Jason Pink had no interest in achieving millionaire status by the time he was 30, nor in becoming a star athlete, performer or inventor. What he did seek was something quite challenging—there being few role models to follow, and the goal itself being such a subtle one that it was hard even to put into words.

How to explain it? Perhaps with a metaphor.

Jason had an inkling that only the flimsiest of veils prevents us from experiencing reality in a dramatically different way, and that if we could only find out how to flick this curtain aside, then we would be able to lead lives with a vivid intensity and rapture that would leave everyday reality behind us in the dust. What did this obscuring curtain consist of? How might one remove it? All Jason had were intuitive feelings to go on. What made him pursue his goal with a relentless intensity was the simple fact that he regularly caught glimpses of what might be possible directly for himself.

From a young age, Jason had had the most amazing dreams. Turning out the light and closing his eyes, several times a week he'd slip into versions of reality immeasurably more sublime than the one he inhabited during the day. He would find himself in landscapes that were in some way familiar, and yet vividly, magnificently more delightful than their daytime equivalents. His dream time encounters with others would touch him so powerfully that he'd continue to experience the wonderful, heartfelt feeling for hours to come. There were even occasions when, for several days, he would be bathed in the afterglow of the love and profound wellbeing his dreams evoked.

Occasionally, it's true, things went the other way. Great, fire-breathing animal-faced monsters would pursue him across hellish landscapes of earthquakes and flames. Fortunately, such experiences were rare.

There was also a recurring dream, which created a curious yearning within him. He would find himself in a verdant garden facing the most luminously wise and loving man with a kindly face and all-seeing eyes, and all he wanted was to get closer to him. The man stood in the middle of an ornate, golden pavilion which Jason sensed was central to every other dimension of reality, but he couldn't get to either the man, or even up the steps of the pavilion, because the whole thing was shrouded in some kind of opaque, paper-like wrapping, covered in words, lines and symbols.

His only consolation came in the form of a dazzling bluebird who would appear from the man's heart, fly unhindered through the indefinable barrier, and land on his left shoulder. As soon as she did, he'd feel so touched by her beauty and wisdom that an ecstatic ripple would flow through him.

Whatever dreams he was having, Jason knew they had nothing to do with his physical body. His eyes were firmly shut and his consciousness withdrawn from his senses when all this was going on. Yet in his dreams he experienced sights, sounds and even visceral sensations much more intensely than when he was awake.

From this he understood that you didn't need a physical body to see, or smell, or endure any kind of experience with an acuteness that was more real than reality. From an early age he deduced that heaven or hell need not be material places so much as states of mind—and no less glorious or horrifying because of that. There were no limits to a mind untethered from form.

These recognitions were accompanied by many questions. Were dreams really nothing more than a by-product of the brain, whirring and clunking its way through the day's events, like some early generation computer? Or was there a different explanation?

What if the places he went to—places with which he was so familiar he could picture them even while awake—had some form of reality? As for himself, the main protagonist of his dreams, sometimes he experienced himself as Jason, but on other occasions he would find he had quite effortlessly morphed into a very different version of himself, or even a different identity altogether, who felt just as real as Jason ever did. Who were these alter egos, whose form he could assume with such ease? Where did the idea of them even come from? Body aside, did his usual idea of Jason have any more substantial reality than the version of himself who had flown across mountains only the night before?

As the son of two schoolteachers, from an early age Jason had been taught respect for scholarship and learning. Knowledge was to be found in books. He had learned that there were few questions you could ask which hadn't been studied already. Which was why discovering what wise beings of the past had to say about such matters became his obsession, one which grew with each passing year as every advance in his understanding produced only a wave of fresh questions.

For all Jason's eager inquiry, he wasn't entirely a geeky bookworm with his nose permanently buried in some abstruse text. It's true that he wore spectacles. And that he had a double degree with distinctions in both mathematics and philosophy. But he was also a good-looking young man whose easy manner and quiet confidence made him popular with the girls.

In the feminine, as in ideas, Jason was drawn to the exotic. Women who didn't conform to a predictable pattern. So it was hardly surprising that he was enchanted by Shivani: a gorgeous Indian woman with dancing eyes and café au lait skin. They had found themselves in the same tutorial class, the subject of which became a private joke: electromagnetics. Attraction generated at an early stage, as the turbines of their romance whirled ever faster, and just months after Jason graduated they decided to move in together.

Jason, who had started work for an insurance company as an analyst after graduating, was still on an intern salary. Shivani was into the second year of a Masters degree in astrophysics. All they could afford was a tiny clapboard cottage with creaking floorboards, plumbing that gasped and wheezed erratically, and a multitude of practical quirks that needed fixing. These included lamps in want of new fuses, latches that required tightening and a myriad other minor irks. Having little patience with practical matters, Jason said he would get around to sorting these things out. As soon as he got the right tools.

Despite the minor inconveniences, the two of them had never been happier, giving all of themselves to each other with the heady fervor of youth, making the cottage their own with little candles in glass holders of a dozen different colors, and Nag Jampa incense, and Indian trance music. In the bedroom, their yin and yang-ness was ecstatically manifest in the way their bodies enveloped and limbs entwined, the dark and the pale, rising and falling in search of ineffable bliss. Outside the bedroom it was the same. They were part of their own intimate and rarefied universe, as they traversed subjects that seemed to hold special meaning for just them.

Shivani would stand at the stove—the one with the down light that needed a new globe—preparing the most delectable curries that they'd scoop off their plates with Peshwari naan bread. As she did, they would talk about her studies, or what Jason had been reading, and in the most curious of ways they sparked off each other whole worlds of ideas.

Jason had already explained how the subjects that he found so absorbing—questions like the validity of dreams, the nature of consciousness—hadn't been considered worthy of study by mainstream Western science until very recently. Since the Renaissance, scientists had focused their attention on the external, measurable world, regarding subjective experience with grave suspicion. In the East, the opposite was true, the greatest thinkers applying themselves to interior, subjective experience with rigor and enthusiasm.

Which was how Jason had come to find himself learning about the adventures in consciousness explored in traditions like Shivani's own, Hinduism, as well as others in the East, such as the Bön and Buddhist practitioners of Tibet.

Shivani wasn't at all religious, but having been brought up in the Hindu tradition she had instincts she was happy to share. Sitting at the small, wooden table in the kitchen—the one with the rickety leg that needed several bolts tightened—Jason would hold forth on the intriguing interplay of ideas as he explored the teachings of Zoroaster and Pythagoras, the Gnostics and the Rosicrucians, the esoteric practices of the Kabbalah and the Sufis.

Scooping up a mouthful of deliciously tangy korma into a corner of naan, Shivani would reach across the table when he'd been talking too much and push her food into his mouth.

"You need to find a teacher," she would tell him, drawing him into a state of delighted silence.

She made the suggestion quite often. And Jason, pondering what she said, would respond in different ways.

"What kind of teacher?" he once asked.

"Someone you connect with."

"But … but … what if I went to a Hindu teacher when what I really needed was a Bön one?"

She shrugged. "Then move to the Bön one."

On a different occasion he had responded, "Teacher? I wouldn't know where to begin looking."

"Then start anywhere."

As they were both well aware, Jason's capacity for online sleuthing was impressive.

But "starting anywhere" wasn't an answer that did it for him. He just shrugged.

"What," Shivani asked, eyes gleaming, "if he's sitting some-where right now, waiting for you to connect?"

Jason regarded her with an indulgent smile, "Now you're just being superstitious," said he.

Jason did come to be inspired by one man in particular. Arthur Ellis had been a student of Albert Einstein, and worked as a theo-retical physicist in both USA and latterly Germany, where he had encountered the Dalai Lama back in the 1970s. Drawn to Buddhist teachings, Ellis had soon identified how the Buddha, two thousand years earlier, had not only offered much the same understanding of reality as quantum physics; he had also suggested a path to access that reality on a personal basis.

Ellis had published just one book on the subject, *Beyond Duality*. It had not been a commercial success, the small press that published it going out of business a short while afterwards. In fact it was purely by chance—if such a phenomena really exists—that Jason even came to know of its existence. One day, burrowing through the subterranean labyrinth of his favorite, second-hand bookstore where all the interesting shelves were to be found—shelves with titles like "Esoteric', "Hermetic" and "Theosophical'—he discovered the faded volume with bent corners and yellowing pages.

"Haven't seen this one before?" he said, handing over five dollars to Clint, the bookstore owner.

Clint, a tall, rake-thin man who wore his steel-rimmed specta-cles on a cord around his neck, shook his head. "Came in yesterday," he said, dryly. "I was starting to wonder where you'd got to."

It was an ongoing joke between the two of them that within hours of Clint acquiring some new and arcane treasure, Jason would visit the shop and unearth it.

"Half a dozen copies on the shelf," remarked Jason.

"Lady brought them, plus a whole lot which went into Physics. Said she's clearing out the study of the author himself."

"This author?" Jason brandished his copy *Beyond Duality*.

Clint nodded. "Seems he ended his days not far from here with his nephew's family. She's the wife of the nephew. Said she's bringing in more stuff of his next week."

Jason had only flicked briefly through his copy of the book. The knowledge that its author had lived not far away gave added piquancy to his new purchase.

That evening, while Shivani was at a seminar, he started on Chapter One and, not for the first time wondered what mysterious process had delivered a particular book into his hands at a particular moment. He found it utterly mesmerizing. And exactly what he needed to be reading right now. Had he come across the book, even six months ago, his eyes might have glazed over. But all he had been reading and thinking about just recently had prepared him so that he found the book irresistibly, wonderfully un-put-downable.

Arthur Ellis had brilliantly drawn together high-level concepts from both west and east in a way that revealed how scientists and meditation masters had arrived at the same understanding of reality. It seemed a delightful paradox to Jason that the search to define the true nature of the external, objective world, and that of interior, subjective experience, had reached exactly the same conclusion. One which was summarized by Ellis in words that were clear—and revolutionary.

Ellis quoted the great physicist, Erwin Schrödinger who said, "Every man's world picture is and always remains a construct of his mind and cannot be proved to have any other existence." And, to match it, Buddha's teaching: "The objective world arises from the mind itself."

According to Sir Arthur Eddington: "The physical world is entirely abstract and without actuality apart from its linkage to consciousness." Which Indian philosopher Ashvaghosha similarly summarized as: "Separated from the mind there are not objects of senses."

Ellis explained how, even though everything outside ourselves seemed to be solid and substantial, the truth was startlingly different. The largest mountain, the strongest steel, was made of molecules, which in turn comprised atoms, and most of an atom was, in fact, space. Not even sub-atomic particles could be claimed as solid matter because all subatomic particles had wave nature, which is to say, they could be either particle or wave, or both at the same time. Which is exactly why Einstein was in the habit of observing that reality is an illusion, albeit a persistent one.

So much of what we take to be substantial is nothing other than space. According to Ellis, if all the truly solid matter in the entire solar system was brought together, it could fit into a thimble.

Jason could hardly believe what he was reading! It all served to confirm the intuitive feelings he'd always had that dreams and everyday reality weren't really so very different—except with a surprising twist. It wasn't that dreams were less illusory than they seemed, but that everyday reality was very much more so. The supposedly solid, material world we all took to be the real deal had all the substance of a stage set—a flimsy confection completely lacking in substance.

That night, when Shivani got home, Jason didn't contain his excitement as he told her about the book. Lying on their bed, all the while she undressed, and stepped into the en suite bathroom, washed her face and got into her pajamas, he told her about *Beyond Duality*, and Arthur Ellis's brilliance and the thing that had especially struck him as he'd got further into the book.

"It's like this book was him wanting to get down all the theory, before explaining the practice."

"Practice of what?" asked Shivani.

"Exploring different realities—especially dreams," he said, before shrugging. "I dunno. It's like he's saying, 'This is the basis of the instructions I'm about to give you.'"

"You think he wrote another book?"

"I couldn't find anything online. But I tell you what. I'm going to do some asking around. I even thought ..." he began, before hesitating.

"Yes?"

"I even wondered if Arthur Ellis might be the guy in my recurring dream."

"You mean," she confirmed, "in the celestial mansion? Behind the maps?"

It was only recently, when the dream recurred, that Jason realized that what kept him from making contact with the source of all wisdom and love was an impenetrable wrapping of road maps.

He nodded.

Shivani switched the bathroom light off and took three steps over to their bed, where she straddled him.

"As I keep saying—" she touched his nose playfully with her left index finger "—you need to find yourself a teacher."

"Oh really?" Reaching up under her pajama top, he savored the silky firmness of her torso before cupping her breasts in his hands. "There are some things I prefer to work out for myself."

"So!" Clutching her arms to her ribs, she trapped his hands beneath them as she laughed. "This is work, is it?"

Jason scanned the small collection of books on the faded Indian rug in Clint's office. "You're sure this is all she brought in?"

The bookstore owner nodded just once.

Jason had been into his store every afternoon, since his last visit, to ask if Arthur Ellis's nephew's wife had brought in the final clearance items from the great man's library. Exactly one week later, she had. And Jason was disappointed by what he'd found. A few well-known physics books. A smattering of Tibetan lamas' texts. Even a collection of paperback mysteries from the 1980s. But nothing of a more personal nature. No notebooks or manuscripts. Certainly no second book.

Jason had, in the meantime, been searching online exhaustively where he'd also hit a brick wall. If only Arthur Ellis had done his main work in the post-Internet age, he thought. He may at least have been able to track down some vestiges of what he'd written after *Beyond Duality*. He was quite sure he would have written something. He had published *Beyond Duality* in his early fifties, and hadn't died until his mid eighties.

Turning away from the pile of generic volumes that lay on the carpet, his attention was snagged by a small, wooden box against which several of the books lay resting. About the size of a large shoe box, it appeared to be an old-fashioned card index box, with a small, brass handle on the front of the drawer. Made from pine, Jason noticed an ink stamp on the side, with Arthur Ellis, followed by a local address. His nephew's?

"The box." He nodded towards it. "Is that for sale?"

Clint shrugged. The woman had used it like a shelf to help carry books in from her car. It had no commercial value. If Jason took it, it would save him a trip to the rubbish bin.

"Personal effects of the author?" Clint's eyes gleamed behind his spectacles as he regarded Jason's still forlorn expression. "Those don't come cheap, you know."

Then after a few moments when the young man was still unresponsive to his humor. "You can have it. Free, gratis. Cash in all those loyalty points we don't give our customers."

"Really? Thanks, Clint!" Jason bent down, picking up the box and turning it over in his hands, thinking how it wasn't what he'd come looking for, but it was at least something.

"A memento of the man himself."

"Of inestimable value," said Clint drolly.

That evening, Shivani spotted the box on the desk they'd set up in a corner of the lounge. Jason told her the story. She picked it up, and tugged at the brass handle, only to find that the empty drawer jammed about a third of the way out. She turned to Jason, eyebrows raised.

"I know," he said. "Not opening."

"Hmm." She tried another tug, before deciding not to force things—the same process Jason had been through several hours before. As she turned the box over in her hands, there came the rattle of something metallic. Studying the bottom of the box, she saw that the base was attached to the frame with six brass screws.

"I'll need to take off the bottom to unjam it," Jason told her.

She replaced the box. "Another one for The Repair List," she said, referring to one hypothesis which Jason had no interest in turning into a reality.

The whole point of the box, really, was the address printed on it— which was how Jason came to be knocking at a particular front door the following afternoon.

The gray-haired woman who answered had a kindly face.

"Oh!" she exclaimed, when Jason told her the reason for his appearance. "You'll be wanting to speak to *my* Arthur, then."

Very soon, Jason was in a chintzy lounge, facing a sofa occupied by a pear-shaped man in his late sixties, who had a pear-shaped face and lips the color of a ripe plum, while the woman who'd opened the door, his wife, Gwen, perched, bird-like, on the arm beside him.

"I hope you don't think this ... inappropriate," said Jason, facing the pair. "But I recently read *Beyond Duality*, which I consider to be a work of genius. I got it from the local second-hand bookstore.

The manager there said that Arthur Ellis used to live with relatives nearby, and I tracked you down."

Jason needn't have feared a cross-examination about exactly how he had found them. The couple was only too glad to have the monotony of retirement interrupted by an evocation of celebrity-by-proxy.

Gwen Dickson confirmed that Arthur Ellis, the author, had indeed spent the last twelve years of his life in a cottage at the bottom of their garden, and that they had only recently, ten years after his death, been able to bring themselves to clear out his quarters because they were planning to move to something smaller.

"The point about *Beyond Duality*," Jason told them, "is that it seemed to set down the basis for a book that would follow. A book, perhaps, more like a manual."

Mr. and Mrs. Dickson exchanged a long glance. Mr. Dickson drew himself up, and seemed on the verge of speaking for the first time when his wife said, "You must have read his book very closely. Because yes, you are right. Arthur didn't speak about his writing very much. But when he did, he used to call *Beyond Duality* his Theory. Followed by a much shorter book, more a brochure, really, he referred to as his Practice."

Jason felt a thrill pass through him at this confirmation.

"May I ask—" he swallowed, his excitement evident in the glistening of his eyes "—what the book is called?"

This time, Mr. and Mrs. Dickson exchanged an even longer glance. Mr. Dickson heaved himself up with his right arm and inhaled heavily. Drawing back his head, he seemed on the very brink of making a pronouncement, about to give voice for the first time in this conversation, when his wife interjected.

"You must realize that my husband and I were very, *very* fond of Uncle Arthur."

Her husband, accepting her as spokesperson without qualms, nodded gravely—not only in agreement with what she said but also, it seemed to Jason, with the direction in which she was heading.

"However, we didn't necessarily go along with all his Buddhist … whats-its."

The husband nodded seriously again.

"Fair enough," said Jason, eager to get any caveats, qualifiers or provisos out the way.

"The title of his book was a bit …" Gwen Dickson glanced about the room, not so much in search of the right word, but the confidence with which to say it. When she met her husband's eyes, they narrowed, urging her to continue.

"… out there," she managed, finally.

"Okay," said Jason, growing desperate.

"It was called, *The Astral Traveler's Handbook.*"

"Wonderful!" Jason beamed. "I love the title! And do you know when it was published?"

"Oh, it was never published." Mrs. Dickson shook her head.

"What?!"

"Arthur didn't come close to that. You see, he lost the manuscript."

Jason grimaced, bringing his hands to his face. Had he been alone he would have bellowed with frustration.

"It happened when he was still living in Germany," Mrs. Dickson explained. "He said it just seemed to vanish overnight."

"He must have been … devastated?"

She chuckled. "No, no! Not Arthur. He was always very calm. Equanimity, he used to call it. Said perhaps the universe wasn't ready for his book."

It was at this point that Mr. Dickson had made his surprise intervention. Leaning forward in his chair, he fixed Jason with an expression of fierce significance, those plum-purple lips quivering as he carefully enunciated just two words, "Lama Tsering."

"Yes," his wife pointed out the window. "Lama Tsering. Local Buddhist center. Arthur used to speak of him most highly. He could probably tell you more about what Uncle Arthur wrote, and all his Buddhist …"

"Whats-its?" prompted Jason.

"Exactly."

Jason went on a downer that lasted the rest of the week. Having confirmed the existence of the tantalizingly titled *The Astral Traveler's Handbook*, only to learn that the author had lost the manuscript, seemed the cruelest of twists. Listless and depressed, it was all he could do to drag himself to work every day. He had certainly lost any appetite for reading.

That Friday afternoon, coming home a different way from usual, he passed a hardware store which had a window display that caught his attention: an impressively large box of tools selling at a hugely discounted price.

"Everything for the DIY Enthusiast In One!" a sign was emphatic.

"Strictly limited stocks" announced another.

Remembering that the leg of the kitchen table had finally, and spectacularly, given way that very morning, Jason felt obliged to go inside and buy the tools he needed if they were to use the table over the weekend.

He spent the following day replacing fuses and globes, tightening latches and sanding away rough edges. For all the easy wins, there were many other jobs where initial intervention led to unexpected and frustratingly time-consuming effort. Shivani did her best to coax and encourage him through the list of repairs, even promising to take him out to dinner that night in her shirt, tie, skirt and black fishnet stockings combo, which he had once confessed, he found irresistible.

Bit by bit he sorted out the more fixable aggravations of their small home, though not without a share of DIY cuts and bruising that was well above average.

It was around 4 pm when his girlfriend tapped something with the shiny, scarlet toenail to which she had only recently finished applying polish, in readiness for their night out.

Jason looked at where she was gesturing. It was the wooden drawer he had brought home from the bookstore, now placed under the desk.

"Nah. Tired," he replied to her unasked question. "Let's just chuck it."

"But it belonged to the great author!"

"Hmph."

Shivani bent down, picked up the drawer and turned it over. "Six screws," she said. "I'll do it myself."

She was searching the toolbox for the right size screwdriver when Jason wordlessly took the drawer from her, placed it on the desk, and with a look of weary resignation began undoing one of the screw heads.

His expression changed after removing the fifth screw. By then, able to swivel the base of the unit in a clockwise direction, he'd found the loose object they'd heard clunking about, rattling between the bottom of the drawer and the casement. It turned out to be a steel bolt. But that wasn't what had been making the drawer jam. *That* had been caused by a thick wad of accumulated papers at the back of the unit, that had gathered and curled, and finally created such resistance that the drawer simply couldn't close.

Jason seized the papers, his mood jolted by a sudden thought. Could it be? he wondered with urgent anticipation. No, that would be too much. Arthur Ellis would have checked out the drawer—wouldn't he?

He peeled open invoices more than thirty years old. Envelopes bearing scribbled lists of grocery items. A yellowing postcard from Singapore. Shivani watched him working his way through the detritus, her expression every bit as intense as his.

And as he worked his way through the papers, one by one, a gathered bunch of pages slipped from the others and fell to the floor. They were folded together and as Jason unfolded the aging pages, he encountered a typewritten title, "THE ASTRAL TRAVELER'S HANDBOOK." And underneath, in modest lower case: "Arthur Ellis'.

Jason and Shivani exchanged electrified expressions. Jason turned over the page by way of confirmation. Here were 54 pages of manuscript. Typewritten. Single line. On both sides of each page. Faded but still perfectly legible. "The End" typed at the bottom of the last page.

"This is …" He fought for the words, shaking his head, placing the manuscript on the desk and grabbing Shivani to him. "Unbelievable! Impossible! Just not happening!"

The two of them twirled and jumped and parted, and hugged again.

"Let's just chuck it!" Shivani reminded him.

They both laughed crazily.

That night, Jason stayed up into the early hours, reading the long-lost manuscript. It turned out to be every much as lucid and instructional as he'd hoped. After *Beyond Duality*, he had been prepared for some heavy intellectual lifting. But the way Ellis described it, the ability to use what he termed "the dream body" to explore other realities was, actually, quite simple.

Thinking of all his own amazingly vivid experiences, Jason read the browning papers with the certain knowledge that everything the author described was true. *This* was what he'd spent his whole life searching for. Instead of being subject to whatever random episodes came up when he went to sleep at nights, with Ellis's help he would direct things. Control that sublime and wondrous reality he knew lay in other realms of consciousness. And then perhaps, who knew, control his experience of this realm?

In the armchair of the small, clapboard house, a single Anglepoise casting its light on the aging pages, Jason felt it was as though Arthur Ellis had written this book especially for him. And he couldn't wait to get started.

He tried that very night. Skipping the chapter on Preliminaries, he went straight to the main practice, reading and re-reading the instructions that clearly outlined how one was to occupy one's mind immediately before going to sleep.

He followed the directions closely. Only next morning, waking up with Shivani, he realized that his sleep had been unexceptional. Studying more during the day, he almost couldn't wait to fall asleep that Sunday night to try out the practices. But again, on Monday morning, he awoke with the recognition that nothing unusual had happened during the previous seven hours.

During the week, he tried again, off and on. Without success. In fact, on the one night he didn't bother, he and Shivani returning home from a concert feeling rather tipsy, within moments of putting his head on the pillow he was in a garden of extraordinarily radiant flowers which not only emitted fragrances, but music too, their luscious chord sequences so poignant that in the dream he was moved to tears by their beauty—a feeling that remained with him after he woke the following day.

Mulling over what was happening, or rather, wasn't happening, Jason returned to *The Astral Traveler's Handbook*, deciding to read it afresh. This time he studied the Preliminaries, in detail, where Ellis couldn't have been more emphatic about the need for initiates, as he called them, to complete purification practices. Without such purification, the author made it clear, adventures in the dream body simply wouldn't happen.

Unfortunately he didn't explain what he meant, exactly, by purification practices but this, decided Jason, was where Google came in. Knowing that Ellis was a Tibetan Buddhist, he searched online, discovering a wealth of purification images, mantras and techniques, including one approach that seemed very mainstream. The practice itself was elaborate, requiring visualization, the recitation of a text, and repetition of a multi-syllabic mantra. Regarding all this with some impatience, Jason took comfort in the fact that, according to several teachers and websites, so powerful was this practice, that it was guaranteed to purify all negativities "in an instant". The effects being so fast, thought Jason, if he spent a full hour reciting mantras, that should do the trick.

But alas, even after sitting in a meditation posture, repeating the tongue-twisting Sanskrit phrases, Jason's efforts at astral traveling were to no avail. Several more nights trying to experience his dream body proved fruitless.

Since the discovery of the manuscript, a question had arisen which Jason and Shivani had discussed. Even though, legally speaking, the manuscript belonged to Jason, if the wishes of its author were to be respected, he should tell others of his discovery. The obvious place to begin, being the author's family.

Returning to the Dicksons, Jason found the couple strangely unexcited by the revelation of his finding.

"How nice!" was all that Gwen said, on behalf of them both. And when Jason offered to return the manuscript to them—he had already taken a copy, of course—he got the same lecture about as fond as they were of Arthur, they didn't go along with all his Buddhist whats-its. It was left to Arthur Dickson to repeat those same two words with the same magisterial importance, "Lama Tsering."

"Yes! Take it to Lama Tsering," chimed Gwen. "He'll know what to do with it."

Which was how Jason found himself being ushered into an audience with the Spiritual Director of the Tibetan Buddhist Center, located a short drive from his house.

Having never met a Tibetan teacher before, he wasn't sure of the protocol. But the moment he looked across the soft-lit room, and met the eyes of the lama, all thought disappeared from his mind except for one singular, startling recognition: *this was him!* The man from the recurring dream he'd had since childhood! The one who stood at the center of the celestial mansion and from whose luminously wise and knowing presence he had always been separated.

Until now.

If Lama Tsering had been standing, Jason wouldn't have been able to help himself hugging him. But as it happened, the teacher was sitting on a meditation cushion on a rug. A wisp of incense smoke curled and twisted with languid timelessness to the ceiling from a single, glowing stick. He gestured a cushion opposite him.

"It's you!" Jason had to say, once seated, and making a fumbling effort to bring his palms together at his heart.

Lama Tsering smiled and nodded. In the pause that followed, the tranquility in the room felt boundless—like something from that other realm of being.

Trying to contain his emotions, Jason's eyes were gleaming as he started with what had brought him here. He explained how he'd found Arthur Ellis's book in a local shop. How he felt it had spoken directly to him. The story of the drawer that wouldn't close and the extraordinary discovery of the manuscript.

From a folder he'd brought with him, he took out the time-worn pages of *The Astral Traveler's Handbook* and gave it to Lama Tsering who received it graciously but also, it seemed to Jason, as though he already knew its contents and considered them to be somehow private.

"I thought I should respect the wishes of Arthur Ellis. Perhaps he would have wanted to have it published."

Lama Tsering smiled knowingly at him, in a way that Jason felt obliged to confess, "I did try his instructions. But they didn't work."

On the other meditation cushion, the lama pursed his lips, for a while the robes around his chest quivering, until he was no longer able to suppress what he was feeling. His face becoming wreathed in mirth, eventually he burst out laughing.

In other circumstances, Jason may have felt annoyed, but such was the lightness of the lama's mood and his compassionate presence, that Jason found himself laughing too, the lama's sense of merriment being so infectious.

It was a while before the teacher recovered. "Yes, yes," he said after a while. "These are very advanced practices, you see? First, there must be a good understanding of the sutras. Only then are initiations possible. And only after initiations can one even begin to explore these practices.

Jason recalled Ellis's use of the word "initiate" and realized that it had a specific meaning. It wasn't just a fancy word for someone who wanted to try astral traveling.

"I did try a purification practice," he said defensively.

"Did you learn that from Lama Google?"

Jason took a moment to understand the question, before nodding. "They quoted some high-powered monk saying that if you did the practice then all negativities would be purified in an instant, and you could attain amazing things."

He shrugged, disappointed at the self-evident falsity of this claim.

Lama Tsering regarded him with a look of such deep benevolence that Jason felt enveloped by the glow of it. Holding Jason's gaze he said, "If consciousness has existed since the beginning of time, for aeons and aeons, then what is one human lifetime?"

In the quiet of the afternoon, in that tranquil room, the lama's evocation of eternity was palpable.

When Jason didn't answer, Lama Tsering raised his right hand and snapped his fingers. "Such is the power of certain practices, that even in one, human lifetime, we can transform our experience of reality. *That* is the meaning of an instant."

Jason shifted on his cushion, beginning to realize that even though he had thought he understood the meaning of what he had been reading, he had been mistaken. The most profound wisdom evidently required an interpreter.

"It is useful to have great respect for learning. But experiencing different dimensions of consciousness goes beyond this. We need a teacher. We must not allow intellectual curiosity, spiritual thrill-seeking get in the way of opening our minds and hearts. Our purpose is not to acquire more knowledge but to attain transcendence."

In Jason's imagination, the image of the map-clad celestial mansion was instantly evoked. Was it true that what had kept him from getting close to his teacher, and the source of all realizations, was an over-reliance on his own pursuit of knowledge? Could it be that he had turned the virtue of a curious mind into an obstacle to spiritual progress? Had he mistaken intellectual inquiry for one involving something very different?

In that same moment, the countless times Shivani had told him to find a teacher sounded like a chorus from the heavens. And the pear-shaped face of Arthur Dickson with those purple-colored lips loomed into his thoughts, pronouncing the only two words he'd ever uttered during his visits: Lama Tsering.

"Buddha taught eighty-four thousand sutras," continued the lama. "In addition there are the tantra traditions. What is right for you in your life? Of all the many teachings, like the rays of the sun, which ones are relevant to you? You could spend lifetimes just trying to read them all. It is for the teacher, the guru, to act as a magnifying glass, to focus the rays on what you need, here and now."

"But how does he know what I need?" asked Jason.

"Because he knows your mind."

"How can I be sure about that?"

Lama Tsering touched his heart. "Best is if you feel some sense of connection. If there is a sign. Also—" he tilted his head to one side "—perhaps he can indicate using skillful means."

Jason contemplated this for a while before unknowingly replying with the same phrase he'd used with Shivani several weeks earlier. "What if there are some things I prefer to work out for myself."

"This is work, is it?" retorted Lama Tsering, with an impish smile.

Jason colored at the reminder of that particular scene.

Then as Lama Tsering continued to regard him with a sparkle in his eye. "If you want to take up golf, learn to drive a car … do you purchase books on these subjects, or do you find a golf coach?

A driving instructor? Inner practices also require the learning of a skill. Why would the process be any different?"

Jason was startled by this simple but indisputable notion.

"You *could* watch an online video from one teacher. And buy an hour with a pro. And cobble together your own idea about playing golf, but—" he leaned forward "—your future is too important for hit and miss. The teacher is the foundation of all realizations, not Lama Google. When your real teacher takes you on as a student, that is a task he accepts until you become a fully enlightened being."

"Does this mean," Jason wanted to clarify, "that the same guru I may have known in my last life is waiting for me in this one?"

Lama Tsering nodded. "Somewhat impatiently."

"I thought that idea was just being—"

"Superstitious," chimed the other.

Jason held Lama Tsering's eyes for a while before saying directly, "I know you from my dreams."

The lama nodded. "Meeting in person is not always possible."

"All my life I've wanted to know how I can experience waking reality the way I experience my dreams."

Lama Tsering nodded, his manner indicating that he was well familiar with Jason's quest. "Dream and reality arise from the same mind, and are not separate from mind. There are two methods to affect how we experience them. One is karma, or creating the causes for future effects. The other is to bring your mind close to that of your guru, who is in the nature of bliss."

"So it is possible to experience every day life with …" How to put into words the incredibly vivid intensity of his dreams? The deeply heartfelt feeling of wellbeing that he experienced?

In the end, he chose the lama's own word: "Bliss? Can we really abide in bliss?"

"Of course," the other smiled.

"And ... the veil that separates us from experiencing bliss?"

Lama Tsering met his eyes, and Jason felt as if he was in one of his dreams right now, as rainbow-colored lights beamed from the monk's eyes and throat and heart, filling him with an unconditional love so radiant that all he wanted was to sit here forever, bathed in the glow of it.

Without the monk needing to say anything, Jason didn't so much hear an answer to his question as feel it. And that answer was: ineffable. Beyond expression. Too great to be described. The only veil between normal reality and this one, he realized in that instant, was conception itself. If we are to experience the boundless radiance of our own mind, the full extent of the oceanic love that we discover ourselves to be, we must first abandon all ideas and constructs, all thoughts we have about ourselves.

The truth is to be found not by acquiring ideas, but by letting them go.

A few mornings later, Jason and Shivani were sitting on the small porch outside their kitchen door, drinking chai. It was something of a weekend ritual when the weather was good. Jason had told Shivani all about his extraordinary encounter with Lama Tsering, and how he had turned out to be the wise man from his dreams. He had also explained his realization that no amount of book reading was going to take him where he wanted to be—he needed instruction from a teacher.

Shivani had resisted any "I told you so's". After the roller-coaster of the past few weeks, she was just happy that Jason, thanks to *The Astral Traveler's Handbook*, had finally begun resolving the questions that had for so long preoccupied him—if not in quite in the way he had imagined.

A mulberry tree grew by the porch, and in the stillness of the morning the two noticed its branches quivering. Then, without notice, from amongst the leaves came a bluebird, which landed on the porch wall, the shortest distance away, taking them in.

Jason and Shivani exchanged sidelong glances, holding their breaths so as not to startle her. They had never had a visitor like this before in their garden—she was simply dazzling, her feathers shiny azure, flecked with black at the wing tips, and darkening to a cobalt at the face. She was so close, they could see light glinting in her eyes as she tilted her head and hopped daintily along the wall. For a while she paused, turning to face them, before fluttering to where Jason had one leg folded over the other. Pausing for the briefest moment on his knee, she cocked her head, looking directly at him before flying away.

"So, is it finally happening?" Shivani's eyes twinkled. "The veil between dreams and reality is falling away?"

"Well, it was an interesting confirmation of the dream I had last night."

"Oh?"

"You know, the one where the bluebird flies through the maps?"

"Reaching you through the veil of conceptuality?" She was nodding.

"Last night she landed on my shoulder, as before. But this time she hopped down my arm. That's never happened before. I put my hand out, flat, for her to perch on. But as soon as she reached it, she turned into someone."

"Who?" Shivani raised her eyebrows in surprise.

"Who do you think?" He kept looking at her.

"Me?!"

"To make any progress you need a teacher. You were the one who kept telling me. And you were right."

"And this morning's visitor?"

Jason nodded, "Came to say goodbye. Little bluebird has done her job."

Shivani held both hands to her mug of chai as she contemplated what Jason was saying. Before she mused, "Well, not quite."

"No?" Jason regarded her keenly, held in the intensity of the moment.

"There's something else that little bluebird would like you to do" she told him, eyes gleaming.

IF ONLY THEY COULD TALK

ONCE UPON A TIME, NOT SO VERY LONG AGO, THERE LIVED A CAT lover named Mavis Davis. Like most members of this species, Mavis wore her love of all things feline as a badge of pride.

The coffee mug on her desk at work was emblazoned with the words "Crazy Cat Lady" in pink capital letters. Visitors to her home would discover a door knocker in the image of a cartoon-like cat with an entirely unnatural grin. So many of her possessions bore the image of a cat that it would have been easier to catalogue those items that were entirely cat-free.

Cats had been part of Mavis's life since she was a girl. But it was only after she and Hank got divorced, and their daughter, Daisy, had left home, that the volume of her ailurophilia—to give it its proper name—ramped right up.

Mavis Davis wasn't some lonely, old crone who had no one on whom to lavish her considerable affection other than her three cats. On the contrary, she lived life to the brim! Her radio alarm would wake her up before six every morning in time for Zumba class at the local gym. She'd return home, charged with adrenalin, chattering volubly to her three fur babies as she bustled from shower to bedroom and from wardrobe to kitchen, where she'd catch the early morning news on TV while she and all three cats devoured their respective breakfasts with lip-smacking gusto.

Her job, as the head of accounting for a busy advertising agency, kept her more than occupied during the working day. And those evenings she wasn't out at an agency do, or enjoying a meal with Daisy or one of the girls from the gym, or dating—yes she had an online profile and had enjoyed some quite delightful dalliances—she spent at home with her cats. Typically, this involved a ready-made meal on a tray in front of the TV, a glass of Merlot, and her phone—those vital components of a pleasant evening home alone. Her phone was a necessary instrument not only for the myriad social media apps she would hop between—Mavis thought of herself as the consummate multi-tasker—but also in case one of the cats struck a particularly adorable pose, which she would capture, caption, and blast out to the world so that all could share in her fulsome appreciation.

Anyone acquainted with Mavis soon also became acquainted with Methuselah, an ancient tabby, and her first rescue cat from the local haven. The vet had estimated him to be at least 12 when she had adopted him 5 years earlier. Methuselah may be a senior, but of all three cats he was also the most generous with his affections, hopping on her lap as soon as she removed the dinner tray, and responding to her chatter and caresses by appreciatively revving up his outboard motor to full throttle.

She'd found Shrek, an off-white cat, starving and bedraggled in an alley behind work. While Shrek had soon bounced back to rude, good health under Mavis's doting ministrations, she suffered from a chronic skin condition that mystified the vet. She lost fur constantly, sometimes in great chunks, especially around her face. At times she'd have so little fur on her head, or the fur that she had was so wispy, that she'd look like she was bald. "So ugly that she's cute!" Mavis would show colleagues photos of the alien-like being on her phone. No doubt some of her co-workers didn't think that Shrek was quite *that* ugly, but they indulged Mavis by keeping their own counsel on the subject.

Despite taking her in and giving her the most loving of homes, Mavis's affections seemed rarely reciprocated by Shrek. In mornings and evenings, as soon as she had eaten, she would vanish into thin air, in the way that cats do. So low was her profile and so rarely seen, that Mavis even gave her the nickname Shrek The Invisible.

Mavis tried her best not to feel disappointed by the cat's seeming lack of interest. Instead, she'd take solace from those random moments, usually in the middle of the night, when she'd become aware of the mostly bald form who had crept up onto the bed beside her and who, on becoming aware that she was no longer asleep, would softly purr.

Ninja, a young, formerly male ginger, brought up Mavis's trio of little darlings. His full name, Ginger Ninja, gave an inkling into his particular character trait, which was to leap out unexpectedly from behind doors and on top of cupboards, and, having startled his prey, scamper away at full speed. Like Methuselah, he was a rescue cat whom Mavis had brought home after she'd fallen in love with him during a visit to the local cat haven—as spontaneous as one of Ninja's own attacks. Opening the door to his rescue center condo, the moment she had encountered Ninja, he had walked towards her and, with the utmost gentleness, head butted her in the heart.

It was a habit that had continued ever since. She'd be sitting at the kitchen bench when Ninja would appear at her side. No matter what she was doing—checking through the mail, drinking a coffee, even eating a meal, he would slip between her and whatever engaged her attention, purring and smooching at her heart. Mavis thought this utterly delightful! Pushing away her mail, or coffee or plate of food, she'd caress her little Ninja and tell him how much she loved him, and adored having him in her life and was so pleased she had found her way to him on that spur of the moment trip to the rescue center.

There were times, in Mavis's hellter-skellter life, when she'd sometimes reflect how she wished she could somehow bridge the human-feline divide. As besotted as she was with her three precious friends, and as much as she showered them with her affections, there was no escaping the feeling that even though they shared the same house, and even the same bed, they lived in different worlds.

In the mornings, she'd sometimes come home from Zumba, bursting with energy and eager to share details of the class, and the day ahead, and what was going on at work with her little darlings, to find all three cats lined up, backs towards her, staring silently out the French doors to the patio. It almost seemed as if they were deliberately blanking her. Many evenings it was just Methuselah and her in front of the TV. What was it about her favorite sitcoms and dramas that Shrek and Ninja found so deeply off-putting?

Perversely, the only time that all three cats seemed actively to seek her out was the one moment that she sought complete privacy: in the bathroom. Soon learning to leave the bathroom door ajar, rather than closed—that would only provoke scratching—as she sat in silence, communing with nature, all three of them would form a procession to the opposite side of the room, where they'd sit, staring at her with sphinx-like inscrutability.

"If only they could talk!" she'd often say to friends, as she showed them a sample from the gazillions of cat pics she had on her phone.

"If only they could talk!" she'd conclude, after telling colleagues about Shrek's most recent hair loss episode. Or Ninja's disturbing new habit of not so much gently head butting her chest, as running full tilt into it like a steam train.

"I'm sure they'd have such interesting things to say."

Mavis had never speculated on what these interesting things might be. On what subjects might one expect a cat to have a fresh and distinctive perspective? The rise of do-it-yourself terrorism? The implications of global warming? The impact of CPI on consumables? Come to think of it now, there are a few.

But as most people understood, the subjects Mavis would really have liked to have conversed to her cats about were of a more personal nature. Like the way they really felt about one another, feline quirks and eccentricities aside. Like what they really would have liked her to do for them. Even what they may have liked to do for her.

If only they could talk.

Mavis may very well have spent the rest of her life speculating on this very question, were it not for an entirely unexpected turn of events: one day, she dropped dead.

Well, slid dead, to be precise.

There she was one minute, attending a weekly agency meeting. And the very next, she experienced two violent spasms in the chest, before slumping against her chair and sliding to the floor. Dead as a doornail.

The colleagues who knew, and for the most part were very fond of Mavis, observed this in a state of benumbed horror. Their disbelief at what they were witnessing seemed to prevent them from moving. Chief Executive Officer, Darius Drake, explaining the benefits of a new invoicing system, was mid-sentence when he saw Mavis flailing. Everyone followed his gaze. And collectively watched her die before their very eyes.

As it happened, an intern named Luke who had joined the agency staff just a few weeks earlier watched the middle-aged woman collapse in front of him without a scintilla of emotion to cloud his reactions. Getting up immediately, he went to the door, opened it, and yelled out, "Kathy! Meeting Room Three. Now!"

So imperative was his tone, that within seconds the agency's First Aid Officer was hurrying to join them.

Although having a heart attack may not strike you, on any level, as being lucky, there were several lucky things about Mavis's. To begin with, where she had it. If she'd been home alone, no matter how well intentioned her cats, she would have been beyond immediate help.

It was also lucky that Luke just happened to be in the staff kitchen two days earlier when Kathy had been telling colleagues about the First Aid refresher course she had just attended. In particular, the very handsome doctor from whom, she had quipped, she wouldn't have minded receiving mouth-to-mouth resuscitation. Luke had been privately disgusted. Kathy couldn't have been a day under forty! The idea that a woman of such an age could still harbor such instincts, much less express them, was something that made him recoil. It had certainly stuck in his mind. Which was why he had no doubt about who to summon when the subject of resuscitation returned to the agenda with unexpected suddenness.

Kathy administered CPR. The Chief Executive Officer, unfrozen, summoned an ambulance. Within half an hour, Mavis was at the city hospital, hooked up to an array of impressive technology, her every metabolic moment being monitored in multi-dimensional detail.

It wasn't until the following day that the whole story emerged. How Mavis had been suffering from high blood pressure without realizing it. How it ran in the family. How the swift response to her situation meant she would suffer no major heart damage. How she would, nevertheless, need to make some lifestyle changes.

"We'll soon have you back to work, and the gym," Mavis's cardiologist had reassured her, on his ward round. "The beta blockers will work their wonders. But we need to find a way for you to better manage stress."

Sitting up in bed in the pajamas Daisy had brought from home, Mavis had felt almost fraudulent being in hospital. And at the same time, terrified. She felt no different from the way she usually did, and was bursting with impatience to be discharged. But on the other hand, an unknown and devastating vulnerability had been exposed. One she was frightened could arise unexpectedly at any moment. There was little she wouldn't have considered to ensure she didn't suffer a repeat of it.

"What do you recommend?" she asked the cardiologist.

"Well, you're not overweight. You've already got a good exercise regime. Your diet could probably do with a bit of tweaking—but it's not that bad either." The cardiologist went through his checklist before studying her closely over the top of his spectacles. "I believe that calming practices like meditation can be helpful. Is that something you would consider?"

"I'd consider anything."

Feeling in the pocket of his white coat, he produced a card, which he handed her.

"'Integrated Wellness Center'," Mavis read aloud.

"They run six week meditation courses for beginners, amongst other things. You may like to give one a try."

From the very first morning Mavis began practicing meditation at home, she noticed a difference. In a way she had never expected.

She felt self-conscious and slightly foolish sitting on her new meditation cushion in the spare room, gazing unfocused at the carpet and trying to count her breaths in cycles of ten, the way Hannah at Integrated Wellness had shown the class. She'd keep losing count of her breath, long before reaching ten. Thoughts would bubble up in her mind. Before she even realized it, she'd be deeply engaged in some subject that was far, far away from breath-counting. Then she'd suddenly realize that she was no longer focused on her breath. For the first time she discovered how little control she had over her own mind.

For all that, something else went on that was unusual in the most delightful way. Within moments of sitting on her cushion, Methuselah appeared in the spare room. She tried to ignore the movement at the door—she was supposed to be focused single-pointedly on her breath—but she couldn't help stealing a glance to where he sat, neat as a pin, staring at her intently.

A few moments passed, and she became aware of another movement. Ninja! He joined Methuselah, sitting upright and staring at his human with the same clear-eyed inscrutability.

Before her first session had ended, Shrek made her appearance too. Standing behind the other two cats and taking in the proceedings, as the three of them looked on, from a distance, Mavis realized what was happening that morning was, quite simply, unprecedented. Apart from her visits to the bathroom, never had all three of her cats presented themselves, voluntarily, while she was wide awake.

She wondered if it was the novelty of it. There's nothing more intriguing to a cat than a slight change to a familiar situation. A piece of furniture moved to a new room. A favorite blanket that has found its way to a different location. A cupboard door, left ajar, that has never been open before. After a few days of meditating, she wondered, would the cats have lost interest?

Next morning, she sat to meditate with an enthusiasm that was only partly to do with the anticipation of oceanic calm. Within moments, Methuselah had not only appeared at the door, but come halfway across the room towards her and settled on the carpet. Ninja and Shrek had soon followed suit, coming quite close to her before sitting, then lying on the carpet. Not wanting to jinx what was happening, Mavis did her best to keep her mind focused on her breath. Her reward, after a few moments, was to hear Methuselah begin to purr.

Mavis arrived at work that day on a high! She shared with colleagues her tale of the unprecedented feline attention she was getting at home. Such was her enthusiasm for the new meditation practice that over the lunch hour she downloaded a Zen chime to her mobile phone to replace the more imperative alarm she'd been using to end her fifteen minute sessions.

And things got only better. The next day, as soon as she was settled on her cushion, Methuselah walked up and helped himself to her lap. Not to be outdone, Ninja came to her side and lay, leaning again her left thigh. Shrek followed, lying directly on the carpet in front of her, at one point even rolling over and stretching out the curved baldness of her tummy.

Mavis had never known such intimacy with her beloved felines. As she sat, trying her very best to keep her mind focused on her breath, she was helped along by the soundtrack of at least two cats, gently purring.

Something was changing in a subtle, but significant way between her cats and her. Something that couldn't easily be put into words. But there was a new closeness, of which physical proximity was the most obvious, but not only, manifestation. For the first time in her life, she experienced the uplifting and yet completely natural sensation that she and her cats were somehow in sync.

The following week at the Integrated Wellness Center she couldn't wait for Hannah to invite questions.

"A kind of weird thing has been happening when I meditate," she told Hannah and her fellow novices. "My cats are coming into the room to join me. A couple of them are usually stand-off-ish. What's all that about?"

Hannah hadn't seemed a bit surprised. "It's by no means unusual," she responded. "My dog waits to join me every morning as well. When we meditate, we deliberately change our mental state. Our body is relaxed but we are focusing our mind on just one thing. This is very different from our usual state of being. You could say that we create a shift in presence, in energy. Research shows how dramatically we change our whole psycho-physical state when we meditate. We produce endorphins instead of cortisol. Our brain waves move to far greater coherence. This is not just touchy-feely stuff—its scientifically measurable. And because animals are more sensitive to non-verbal changes than we are, they instantly pick up on what's happening. Many of them are drawn to us."

Mavis swallowed, humbled by the perceptiveness shown by her beloved cats. "I feel like I'm somehow on the same page as them. Almost as if they might speak."

Hannah regarded her closely for a few moments before saying, "Animals use sound to communicate, but they routinely use more subtle signals … what we might call knowingness, intuition, telepathy. People who live close to nature do this too. My personal belief is that all humans used to communicate like this once, but our minds have become so busy that, for the most part, we're incapable of picking up subtle signals any longer. We have so much noise in our lives—TV. Radio. Social media. It's very interesting what happens when we step away from all that and learn to let go of cognitive chatter and simply be with our pets. Once the barriers go, communication flows."

"You're saying," prompted another class member, "we can communicate with animals this way?"

"Not verbally," replied Hannah. "But when we quiet our minds and open up to what they may be trying to tell us through their actions, perhaps even through symbols—it's amazing what we discover. A lot of pet lovers say that they're always talking to their animals, but the reality is that it's mostly one-way traffic." She smiled. "Talking to our pets is one thing. But do we ever stop to listen?"

Mavis left her second meditation lesson in a state of deep unease. She was exactly the kind of pet lover that Hannah had been describing. All these years it had been one-way traffic! Her chattering to the cats about her day at the office. Her dominating the sound waves with TV and online videos and noise without end. But the moment she had offered her beloved felines some peace and quiet, they had responded to it with unprecedented appreciation.

How could she have got it so very wrong for so many years?

She, a cat lover of all people?!

That night, for the first time ever, she didn't switch on the TV when she got home. Instead, she and the cats enjoyed their dinner in silence. And, was she imagining things, or did Ninja and Shrek hang around for longer before they did their usual vanishing act?

In the days that followed, Mavis tried to put her relationship with her cats onto a new footing. Their morning meditation sessions now an assumed part of their daily routine, Mavis added a short,

session of contemplative silence before turning out the light each
night—and the result was a full complement of cats on the duvet
beside her. She made an effort to reduce the noise levels at home,
investing in a set of headphones so she could watch TV without
filling the place with sound. She was rewarded, very quickly, when
Ninja and even Shrek proved to be less elusive.

But, as important as any of this, she began to listen. To pay
attention. To ask her cats if there was anything they wished to tell
her, and then to simply wait, patiently, to see what turned up.

Her first discovery was both shocking and embarrassing. And it
wasn't even an intentional act of communication, as far as she could
tell. One evening, she called each one of the cats by name. Ninja
and Shrek turned around the moment they heard her. Methuselah,
further away, didn't react at all.

That got her thinking—and setting up a few tests that quickly
confirmed her gathering suspicions: Methuselah was profoundly
deaf. He could hardly hear a thing, unless the sound was right
beside him.

Mavis mused about all those evenings on the sofa, just her and
Methuselah. Was the reason he had joined her because he, alone
among the cats, was inured to the sound of canned laughter, TV
drama sirens and the incessant, bellowing retail advertising? How
long had he been as deaf as this? And what did it say about the kind
of attention she paid him, that she had missed it?

A trip to the vet established that the cause of his deafness wasn't purely on account of his old age. A judicious de-waxing of the ears helped him regain some of his hearing.

A week or two later, Mavis was sitting at the kitchen bench, eating dinner, when Ninja hopped onto the counter, strode over towards her, rubbing his face affectionately against her arm.

"That's very nice, little Ninj." Mavis stroked him. "I love you too."

After more head rubbing and gentle purring, he hopped down onto a stool and began to wash his face.

More sensitive to her cat's behavior, and free of other distractions, Mavis watched him for a few seconds before saying, "It's a while since you head butted me. Not since hospital, in fact. Before I went in, you always used to …"

Which is when it suddenly struck. Only recently had she read about the ability of some animals to detect symptoms of illness among humans. Cats had prodded the abdomens of owners who had stomach cancer. Dogs alerted their diabetic owners to plummeting sugar levels. Horses were able to help veterans suffering from Post Traumatic Stress Disorder—all without a word being spoken.

Mavis remembered her visit to the cat haven. How Ninja's first act had been to head butt her heart. Gently. How he'd continued doing so, with increasing vigor. But, because she hadn't been listening, his warnings had been to no avail. If she had listened, and taken herself off for a simple blood pressure check, was it possible she could have avoided the heart attack altogether?!

The idea that Ninja had been patiently persisting for all these years, to give her a message about her own physical wellbeing, a message that had been in her own, imperative self interest, and that she had been so utterly self-absorbed that she'd been impervious to it, shook her to the core.

There was also transformation in the life of Shrek, albeit of a slower growing variety. After Mavis cut down the noise levels when she was home, Shrek became a more constant presence. Yes, she had been fleeing TV! She was not only physically present, but in a way Mavis couldn't put into words, more emotionally available too. There were encounters, purrs, glances that confirmed things were somehow different.

There was fur, too. At first so few wisps that Mavis didn't dare hope too much. But as the wisps burgeoned into tufts, and tufts started joining together, there could be no further room for doubt.

Previously, following exhaustive tests, the vet had once told her that Shrek's baldness may be a stress reaction, but to exactly what he couldn't say. As Shrek became a gorgeously fluffy white cat, with a full head of hair, there was no question in Mavis's mind about the cause of her hair loss. She was a sensitive cat. And a quiet one. Not for her the hyper-stimulation of twenty-first century life. Offered the simple things—nourishing food; a safe, quiet home; the love of a crazy cat lady—and she flourished.

How frustrating, Mavis began to think, to be a pet. To try telling people things when their capacity to listen was so limited. To suffer, right in front of the eyes of those who loved you, because they were oblivious to even your basic needs. To try drawing attention of those you cared for to something that threatened their very existence, but despite your repeated efforts, to do so in vain.

One day, Mavis emerged from her shower to find the cats lined up at the French door, backs towards her, staring into the patio. Their meaning, she recognized now, could hardly be plainer.

She opened the door to the courtyard, and all four of them stepped into a spring morning. Usually, she meditated in the spare room, but that morning she brought a chair outside, and sat in her bathrobe, and was simply present to her senses.

It was one of those delightful, pristine moments when the world felt as though it had been freshly minted. A morning breeze carried with it scents of crocuses and freesias. Birds trilled mellifluously from trees in the park nearby. The sun felt warm in Mavis's face as she sat, being here and now.

Methuselah didn't sit on her lap that morning, but rather perched on a small step, bathed in the sunlight. Beside her on the pavers, Shrek sprawled out, getting maximum exposure to the warmth along the full stretch of her white, furry tummy. Ninja prowled through the small flower bed nearby, like a jungle beast.

It didn't matter where they all were that morning, physically. In a more important way, they were all exactly where they wanted to be, and in those peaceful moments of radiant wellbeing, they had never felt closer.

All of it, the cats' idea.

A few weeks later, a colleague of Mavis's in the graphic design team approached her in the lunch room to show her images of the kitties she had just adopted from her local rescue center. Like everyone else in the office, Cathy knew that Mavis was a cat tragic, as Darius Drake ironically termed it.

A group of colleagues were soon clustered round Cathy's phone as she flicked through images of her two adopted kitties. The cats were already displaying markedly different personalities as well as enigmatic quirks, such as a lust for buttered toast.

"If only they could talk," said a woman from accounts, to murmurs of agreement. "Isn't that what you always say, Mavis?"

"Used to." Mavis nodded. "But, you know, I've completely changed my mind about that. Cat's *do* talk. They are communicating with us the whole time. The more important question is, do we ever listen?"

That night, as Mavis lay in bed waiting for sleep, she recalled her conversation with Cathy. She thought of all the years, while claiming to be besotted with her cats, she had unwittingly ignored them, being deaf to their pleas for peace, their wish for contact with nature. She had been closed off to the possibility of the silent but profound communion she had only just begun to experience, but which had already transformed things between them.

She thought of all the other pets around the world whose lives were similarly constrained by the tragic unawareness of their owners. All those missed opportunities for the freedom and the profound well-being she had only recently discovered. For the experience of wordless acceptance, and of love. And as she reflected, a rush of such deep sadness welled up inside her that she let out an involuntary sob.

Lying on her side, she wondered how things could ever be changed? How was it possible to share with every pet lover the full significance of the relationships they could enjoy with their companions, if only they could quieten their minds?

As she lay there, she sensed a stirring on the bed, and the shadow of a once-bald but now luxuriantly fluffy cat fell over her. And, in the next moment, the sandpapery quality of a small, pink tongue licking her cheek.

WAKING UP IN THE CITY MORGUE

WHEN CATHERINE TURNER LOOKED IN THE MIRROR, SHE WAS DISAPPOINTED by what she saw. The 52-year-old woman returning her gaze had a sagging jawline, deeply etched crow's feet, and a puffiness under the eyes that never fully went away. Stepping back—something she avoided doing when naked—it was to be confronted by the same, grim effects of aging writ large. She'd be startled if she ever caught an unguarded glimpse of her own reflection in a shop window. Even though her journey into middle age had been as gradual as everyone else's, she was always jolted by the reminder of how she really looked. Because it was nothing like the much younger version of herself that existed in her mind.

How to deal with the rush of thoughts and feelings that came to the surface at such moments? For Catherine there was a phrase that summed it up. "Gracious acceptance" was her chosen philosophy. Gracious acceptance of the fact that, with every year that went by, her very best days were receding further and further into the past.

She'd be needing all the gracious acceptance she could muster this morning, she thought wryly, surveying her wardrobe. The first cupboard contained her expensive items—some designer garments, pretty dresses she had bought for a holiday or silk items that needed to be dry cleaned instead of washed—things she thought of as too special for every day. The third cupboard had round-the-house clothes, and once treasured garments she no longer wore, but which she couldn't bear to part with.

It was the second cupboard she was looking in now, the cupboard of new-ish outfits. Clothes that weren't anything special, but that were perfectly presentable. The kinds of clothes worn by invisible, middle-aged women when they went out to lunch with their invisible, middle-aged friends.

Being the first Friday of the month she had a standing lunch arrangement with two girls from school days. Same time, same place. It had been the same for several years, but she sometimes wondered why, because every time they met they just seemed to go over the same conversational ground.

Marta, a landscape artist who had enjoyed brief commercial success in her early forties, lived on an emotional roller coaster of pie in the sky fantasies followed by crushing disappointment, and had little real interest in anyone except herself.

Meantime, there was nothing you could tell the super-chilled Briana that could surprise her, and she had an irksome habit of continually asking after Catherine's brother, Gerry, who she'd had a crush on as a teenager—one that seemed to have resurfaced late in life. Every second or third lunch Briana would ask if she'd been in touch with Gerry, and every second or third lunch Catherine would have to tell her the same thing: "no."

Gerry's wife had estranged him from the rest of the family, and Catherine had had no contact with her brother for over a decade. Although she had heard, via the grapevine, that Gerry and the toxic wife had parted company about a year ago, she knew nothing more because he lived in another city, and they had no mutual friends. Growing up, she and Gerry had been particularly close and he was her only sibling. Deeply wounded by his inexplicable withdrawal, as far as she was concerned it was now up to him to signal if things had changed.

A third friend used to come to their lunches—and brighten up their lives with her irresistible *joie de vivre*. May Delaney had combined the sweetest of temperaments with a sparkling sense of humor—enough to make Marta forget herself, and Briana melt out of her brittleness. But May's husband, Stanley, had been transferred to the Bahamas, and they had been gone for three years. During this time May had frequently pleaded with Catherine to go out and visit for an extended holiday, an idea that, on the one hand, thrilled Catherine but, on the other, she didn't feel ready for.

Klaus's heart attack, two years ago, had left Catherine a widow at a relatively young age and she was still coming to terms with life on her own. It was true that neither of her very busy, married sons seemed to have much need for her. And having retired early she had no career to think of. But for reasons she couldn't quite put her finger on, reasons, she supposed that had to do with clinging to the familiar and the known, the idea of a long-haul flight on her own to the other side of the world, even to be with May, felt like a step too far.

Catherine had a deep-down inkling that she was living in an ever-diminishing world. Still inchoate and unexpressed, it was a sense that would register briefly from time to time that if she wasn't careful, her life would shrink and narrow to the point where the comfort of the familiar became increasingly uncomfortable. When any changes to her routine would come to seem like upheavals, and the smallest of molehills take on the dimension of mountains.

Little did she realize, as she settled on an outfit from the second cupboard—dark pants and a jacket with a soft, cotton scarf to provide a splash of color—that she was about to find salvation that very morning.

She was walking along a pavement to her lunch date when a man in a motorized wheelchair appeared round the corner, hurtling forward at such speed that pedestrians had to throw themselves out of his path. In Catherine's case, she abruptly found herself shoved against a shop window by a schoolgirl falling against her legs.

In the moments after the wheelchair had passed, while those around her, including the girl, peeled themselves off each other and back onto their feet, Catherine's cheek was pressed against the window of the shop, which turned out to be a recruitment agency. On the other side of the glass, a neatly printed card read, "Admin Assistant—City Morgue. Two-week contract."

Before retiring, Catherine's working life had been as a paralegal, a job demanding both admin as well as legal skills. That's how she and Klaus had met thirty years ago. At the time, he had been an up and coming young lawyer, and she had been an attractive and vivacious addition to the paralegal pool. Both working in the area of medical law, during the decades that followed, there were few aspects of human biology that hadn't been the focus of one case or another.

Biology had been a subject of special interest to Catherine since the time she'd been first introduced to it at school. While many others in her class were repulsed by the workings of the human digestive tract, Catherine had found it intriguing. Some of her fellow students had shielded their eyes from school documentaries about bilharzia or gonorrhea, but Catherine had found them deeply fascinating. And it was gruesome medical errors and biological abnormalities that had been the sweet spot in her otherwise desiccated work of a paralegal—one of the few things about her job that she missed.

During her time at university, needing to earn some money, she'd worked for the father of a friend who owned an undertaking business. For several years, she had been quite used to dealing with corpses, and the matter-of-factness with which undertaking staff had gone about their business had soon rubbed off on her.

Within a minute of having her face shoved against the shop window, Catherine was inside the recruitment agency, her entirely uncharacteristic spontaneity prompted by a sudden and powerful curiosity.

"The City Morgue job." She pointed to the window behind her. "Is it still available?"

The angular-looking woman on the other side of the desk regarded her without enthusiasm. "I'd have to check," she said.

The recruitment agent had spoken to her client, Claudio, the afternoon before. He was desperate. The problem was that the window advert was deliberately vague. They had discovered in the past that they wouldn't get a single applicant if they advertised what the job *really* entailed. So instead, they put up a bland "Admin assistant" notice, and tried to find some compliant twenty something who wouldn't object as and when the full truth came to be revealed.

The woman standing in front of her did not belong to that category. If anything, she gave the air of being decidedly non-compliant.

"Can you check now?" asked Catherine, nodding towards the phone on her desk, thereby confirming her unsuitability.

The woman looked at her evenly, making up her mind about something, before saying, "The job involves more than only paperwork."

"Go on."

Detecting the glint in Catherine's eye, the other woman shifted in her seat. "The candidate would have to help with … bodies."

"Really?" Now Catherine was very interested.

"After they've been dissected."

"You mean, post-mortem stitching?" Catherine practically beamed.

"You've done this work before?"

"Never. But I've always wanted to!" In fact, this was the first time Catherine had ever considered spending her days stitching up cadavers but, as the words tumbled out of her mouth, she felt them to be true.

The recruitment agent's eyes narrowed. "They're only offering eighteen dollars fifty an hour."

Catherine shrugged. "Neither here nor there."

The other woman picked up her phone and hit speed dial.

Catherine started work the following Monday. Up till then, she had never given much thought to the whereabouts of the City Morgue, and she was surprised to find it directly opposite the food court in a popular shopping mall. The pungent aroma of deep fried chips accompanied her as she made her way along a corridor opposite the fast food outlets, through a pair of anonymous swing doors, and into a bland reception area in which she had to press a buzzer for attention.

Soon, she was shown into the presence of Dr. Claudio Agostini, Chief Forensic Pathologist. A slim man about the same age as her, his completely shaven head and steel-rimmed glasses gave him a cerebral presence. He also had the most observant eyes—which, she supposed, was central to the work that he did.

In just five minutes he had explained why she was needed—the illness of a staff member; what she was to do—paperwork for a variety of cases and post-mortem stitching for some of them; and where she would wash off—something, he assured her, that would soon become imperative.

The only question he asked her was why, given her impressive paralegal career, she had wanted this particular job. He was amused when she explained her interest in biology.

Dr. Agostini may be all business, that gleaming, bald head of his seeming to pulse with intelligence, but Catherine warmed to him, all the same. There was a certain lightness, even jocularity about him that seemed incongruous given the nature of his job. She had already been told that Dr. Agostini had a team of five forensic pathologists reporting to him, two here and three at hospitals across the city. Plus a supporting team of administrators. It occurred to her that he could easily have asked one of his colleagues to take her under his wing. That he chose to do so himself made her wonder.

She spent her first morning reading up on procedures, watching induction videos and signing confidentiality documents. It was only in the afternoon when she was asked to go to the change room, pass through a foot bath and dress in suitable gowns, gloves and boots.

"All ready?" Dr. Agostini looked at her over the top of his face mask as she joined him. Earlier, he had offered to let her watch an autopsy, so that she could get a better idea of the whole process.

"Nothing quite like your first corpse," he said.

"A very special first corpse," she replied.

He raised his eyebrows.

She tapped the clipboard she was required to carry, with details of the deceased. "We were born on exactly the same day."

She'd made the discovery only a few minutes earlier, and had double-checked it several times since.

"Hmm," he mused. "That's happened once or twice for me. Makes you think …"

"That it could just as easily be me?" prompted Catherine.

"Exactly," he said, bringing a remote control out of his pocket and pressing a button. The room was filled with classical piano music.

"Chopin." She smiled with recognition.

"First piano concerto." He glanced at her with approval. "A favorite."

"Mine too."

The cadaver on the brightly lit table wasn't nearly so ghoulish as the images she'd seen on TV. Pallid and lifeless, of course, but not a blue-skinned horror. There was only the slightest muskiness, a locker room smell, along with the clinical tang of disinfectant.

The woman had had a good figure, observed Catherine, much better than her own. She was slimmer and looked as though she had been fit and supple. Glancing at that lifeless face, the disheveled hair, it was hard to tell how she would have reacted, had they encountered one another in the street. But from the look of her smooth hands and manicured fingernails, the woman had been well presented.

"Deceased two days ago?" queried Dr. Agostini, taking a scalpel from an assistant who had been waiting for them at the examination table.

"Yes." Catherine didn't need to double-check the paperwork. It had already occurred to her that the same afternoon she'd been lunching with Marta and Briana, this woman could have been sitting at the very next table, little knowing that, within 24 hours, she would be dead.

Catherine watched in fascination as Dr. Agostini made bold Y incisions from the shoulders, under the woman's breasts, and down to her naval.

She knew that post-mortems were only required in cases of sudden death, or where there was something suspicious or unnatural, or in cases of accidents or medical errors. She'd read countless reports over the years when she was a paralegal.

Dr. Agostini was methodical, efficient and moved with speed of practice. For her benefit, he also offered a few pointers about what he was doing.

"Middle-aged female, living alone, unexpected death. Had the appearance of being in good health. In cases like this I always check the heart first."

He had opened up the abdomen and reached inside, taking her heart in his hand, and leaning to inspect it under the dazzling light.

Once again, Catherine couldn't help thinking how, only two days earlier, that heart had been pumping at somewhere around 80 beats per minute—or possibly much faster if the woman had been on the cross-trainer at her local gym. She would have had plans for the rest of the weekend. Perhaps this was going to have been just another week, or maybe she was having to face up to something highly stressful? Whatever the case was, for her, the week had never come.

Had she had any warning? Would she have known, even a minute or two before she finally died, that she was about to lose her life?

Catherine didn't realize that she had asked the question out loud until Dr. Agostini returned the woman's heart to her chest.

"In the case of myocardial infarction, it can vary," he answered. "Often there is severe chest pain. There may be varying degrees of recognition about what's happening. Sometimes the signs are so minor that people don't even know they've had a heart attack. They may think it's just indigestion. Anyway, that wasn't the scenario here. Next stop, the brain."

"Stroke?" queried Catherine.

"That's what we'll check for."

She glanced at his surgical instruments, wondering how he was going to open the skull.

Instead he turned to nod to his assistant, who flicked a brake on a wheel Catherine didn't know existed, then began pushing the whole table, cadaver on top, across the examination room towards swing doors.

"MRI," Dr. Agostini told her.

"You don't have to saw the head open?" she asked.

"Not generally. We're looking for atherosclerosis of extracranial or major intracranial arteries. Dissection can muddy the waters."

In the next-door room, the cadaver was placed on a conveyor belt and loaded into the machine where scans were taken. They revealed that the woman had, almost certainly, suffered a massive stroke.

Back in the examination room, the assistant showed Catherine how to stitch together the tissue Dr. Agostini had cut open. Skin, muscle and soft tissue was very different from working with felt and curtain fabric, the only things that Catherine had stitched in her life. But she focused intently, followed instructions, and worked through it. She was aware, all the time, of the oozing of subcutaneous fat out of the cadaver. It seemed to liquefy and slide from the incisions across the skin onto the examination table and seep across her gloves and protective clothing. And with it a floral aroma, somewhat sickly.

Even in the temperature-controlled City Morgue, the odor of decomposition was unavoidable.

That evening, Catherine's elder son, Jamie, phoned her after supper.

"How was your first day at the morgue?" he asked. Jamie was as amused as all her other friends by what he termed his mother's "macabre side".

"Interesting," she said. She had stitched four cadavers that afternoon. It was the first that was most vivid in her mind, not only because it had been her first, but also because of the shared birthday. Telling her son about the coincidence, she recollected how, on leaving the building that afternoon, she had been about to cross the street when Dr. Agostini had appeared up the ramp from the basement car park, behind the wheel of a bright-yellow Porsche.

She'd smiled. "Nice car!"

He'd pulled up beside her, the driver's window wound down. "My indulgence," he'd replied, eyes twinkling.

From inside the car, she'd heard the sound of orchestral music and she'd had the sudden recognition, in that moment, that in an important way, Dr. Agostini knew how life should be lived.

Moments later, he had taken off, the engine of the car unleashing its distinctive, throaty roar.

Later that week she had to stitch together the corpse of a young girl whose face she had recognized immediately—it was splashed across billboards, bus shelters and shop windows throughout the country. An eighteen-year-old model who was the ambassador for a well-known clothing chain, she had been found dead after a heated row with her boyfriend at his apartment. Catherine had seen a news item on TV about the death, little thinking that she would encounter the naked form of the famous model on the examination table at work.

Conducting the post-mortem, Dr. Agostini tut-tutted as he sliced open that famous body, to study its gastric contents—blood and urine samples being already subjected to drug screening. Lethal drug toxicity, he told Catherine, was sometimes very difficult to establish. Drug use, albeit of the legal varieties, was so prevalent that about a half of all post-mortem cases showed positive for some level of toxicity. Knowing the history of each case could be critical in proving if particular drugs, or a combination thereof, had caused death.

Catherine, whose work as a paralegal had included insurance cases for the body parts of models and sports people, couldn't help a certain consternation as she watched Dr. Agostini smoothly open up the girl's torso and reach inside it as though rifling through a handbag for a lost set of keys. But the girl was no longer a fashion model, she had to remind herself. She wasn't even a person.

At the moment of her death, she had been reduced to a medical curiosity.

One with her own particular acrid aroma, she noted. Stunning as the young woman had been, in all the posters and screenshots, three days after death, she was rotting from the inside, and the odor of decomposing human flesh was unmistakable.

As confronting as the scent was the hideous discoloration Dr. Agostini revealed when he opened up the girl's chest cavity: the windpipe was seared brown and the lungs oozed black tar. Catherine had looked from the famous, pristine beauty of the girl's youthful face, to the congealing sludge in her burned lungs. The contrast could hardly have been more striking.

"Smoker," Catherine found herself saying.

"Fairly typical damage," responded the pathologist, pragmatically.

Catherine nodded.

"What seems the most perfect specimen may conceal a multitude of horrors. You can never tell from the outside what's going on inside."

The rest of Catherine's week went by in a combination of post-mortem work and administration. During the course of the latter, she identified duplications in City Morgue systems and got approval to eliminate them. By her twentieth corpse, she was also making headway with her stitching.

Come Friday evening, she felt somewhat disappointed to be already halfway through her assignment. Like the mid-point of a holiday, she had the sense of more stimulation to be experienced—along with the recognition that, before she knew it, the temporary contract would be over.

Meeting friends for dinner that Saturday night, and socializing at the tennis club on Sunday, as she answered all the wide-eyed questions about what went on at the morgue, she told and re-told the story of the corpse with whom she'd shared a birthday. The young girl—professionalism forbade her from revealing the identity—whose apparent, youthful beauty couldn't have been more sharply contradicted by the grotesque contamination of her lungs.

And as she told the stories, Catherine realized that her five days at the morgue had been about a lot more than the experience of mere coincidence or the startling disconnect between outward appearance and inner reality. What had begun as simple curiosity—'morbid fascination,' Jamie would have said—had led to something else shifting. What exactly, she couldn't yet put into words, but she felt it. It was a gathering recognition, a rising tide which she sensed had a deeply personal significance.

The night before her second week at the morgue, she sat at the small writing desk in the corner of the sitting room. Opening the drawer, she glanced across the neatly arranged stacks of cards, printed stationery and deluxe, specialty writing paper.

Catherine had always loved the act of writing with a fountain pen on fine quality paper. When she and Klaus had traveled to places like Venice, Paris or Amalfi, they'd always linger in stationery stores, where she'd select a few of the more irresistible items: items that remained in her desk, waiting for a suitably momentous occasion to be used. They filled more than half the wide desk drawer. Now, as usual, she reached over for one of the free notepads that estate agents sometimes dropped into her letterbox. Hers was an automatic reaction. Long ago she had decided that there was no point using expensive stationery for mundane correspondence:

"Dear Ludwig and Simona," she wrote to her house cleaners, whose twice-monthly visit was due the next day. "I won't be at home today. Please can you polish the mirrors in the hallway and bedroom?"

She signed the note and added a smiley face, before leaving the note on the kitchen bench, along with the usual cash payment.

On week two, Catherine had to sew together the bodies of six children who had been killed when their school bus was T-boned, around the same time she had been playing tennis. There was also the corpse found floating in water, the stench of which no amount of washing or rinsing seemed to eliminate. Perhaps because she was becoming inured to the cases she had to deal with, instead of any one cadaver making a singular impression, as the days went by she was struck by something else: the number of cases for whom the cause of death was one thing, but who would have faced some other medical crisis had they lived very much longer. Many of them, around the same age, or even much younger, than her.

There was the forty-something man who had died of a heart attack thirty minutes after meeting with his accountant. The post-mortem established the formation of a blood clot causing myocardial infarction. It had been further revealed that his abdomen hosted several large, malignant tumors to which the man had, apparently, been oblivious. He had been living with Stage 4 cancer and had been completely unaware of it.

Then there was the young woman killed in a car accident. The force of collision had fractured her skull, ribs and vertebrae, causing extensive internal bleeding leading to death. As it turned out, she had also been on the brink of acute liver failure, which would have seen her delivered to the emergency ward of the local hospital, had she lived very much longer.

As Catherine left the morgue each afternoon and made her way through the food court, the insidious odor of subcutaneous fat roiling and merging with the more pungent aroma of deep fried chicken nuggets, she sensed a return of the feeling that her temporary work at the city morgue had done more than refresh her curiosity about human biology. It was also causing the tectonic plates of her world to move in ways she was only starting to define. In particular, she had come to recognize two strong and contradictory sensations.

Day after day, as she encountered the cadavers of yet more people, very often younger than herself, laid out on the examination table, she had become acutely aware of just how fragile life was. How very easily it could be taken away at any moment.

Who was to say that her own abdomen wasn't filled with grotesque-looking tumors, or that she wasn't on the brink of some other life-threatening crisis? If her work at the City Morgue had taught her anything, it was that you could tell nothing from outward appearances.

None of the people whom Dr. Agostini had sliced open so meticulously had woken up, on a morning during the previous week, knowing that they had only hours to live. They'd no doubt expected just another day ahead, perhaps during another unremarkable week, month or year. And yet it had turned out to be the very last day of their life.

Along with this sobering, but unavoidable recognition, was another, quite unexpected sensation: it was a feeling of lightness. Without realizing it, she had burdened herself with the assumption—incorrect as was now all too evident—that she would still be alive in thirty years time. That life's pleasures were to be eked out. That joy must wait. That fulfillment, resolution and closure could be constantly postponed to some point in the mythical future. Instead of celebrating all that she had to live for, right now, she was coming to realize that she had unknowingly worked her way into a well-worn rut based on beliefs that were just plain wrong.

On her last afternoon at the City Morgue, Dr. Agostini sent a message asking to see her before she went. She knocked on his door shortly before 5 pm.

"Ah—Mrs. Turner." He waved towards the chair opposite. "Already it is time to say goodbye."

She smiled, meeting those perspicacious eyes.

"Has your interest in human biology been satisfied, to some extent, in these past two weeks?"

She paused before saying, "I've certainly learned a great deal."

"Good." He nodded. Then leaning forward, he placed his elbows on the desk, forming a temple with his fingers and touching his chin. "Would you be interested in learning more? I ask for purely selfish reasons. Your maturity and professionalism have been an asset to our team. From time to time, when we need extra cover, it would be helpful to know that we could ask you back."

Catherine had already guessed that Dr. Agostini might pose such a question.

"I think I've seen all I need to satiate my curiosity," she replied. "And the smell of subcutaneous fat …"

"Nothing to recommend it," he conceded. Leaning back in his chair, he seemed resigned to her response. "And the work can be confronting, yes? All those body fluids. Decomposition."

"Discovering that our lives dangle by the most fragile thread."

He nodded. "There are certainly more causes for us to die, at any given moment, than most people care to contemplate."

"But in another way—" Catherine met his gaze "—I have found the experience strangely liberating too."

He raised his eyebrows.

"It has made the reality of my own death much more real. More normal. Matter of fact. I've come to see that it can happen at any moment. And in a strange kind of way, it's like a burden I wasn't even aware of has been lifted from my shoulders."

The pathologist's spectacles glinted as he tilted his head in agreement. "First face death, then we know how to live?"

"If we assume we're going to go on forever," she went on, "we're not really living."

"*Carpe diem*. Seize the day."

"Is that why you drive the Porsche?"

Dr. Agostini tilted his head to one side. "No one has ever asked me that question quite so directly—" he chuckled "—but yes. Yes, it is. I know it may seem a little child-like. But I love the car, and I have the chance today. Who is to say I will have the chance tomorrow?"

For a long while they held each other's gaze across the desk, before Catherine said, "I can honestly say this has been the most life-changing experience since I lost my husband."

"In a positive way, I trust?"

"Very positive. It's been just what I needed to get me out of my rut. I feel strangely, gloriously lighter, which is why I would be very happy to cover any future staff absences."

"Wonderful!" Dr. Agostini beamed at this unexpected conversational turn. Considering what she'd just said, he asked, "A regular reality check?"

"Exactly." She nodded.

"I have no doubt that most people would benefit from the same thing."

Catherine began making changes that very evening. Pouring her favorite Sauvignon Blanc into one of the special wine glasses she only usually brought out for dinner parties—and the last of those had been when Klaus was still alive—she sat on her sofa, picked up her phone and pressed a favorite contact.

Moments later, in the Bahamas, May Delaney answered her call.

"Lovely to hear from you, Katie!" she enthused. She was the only one who called Catherine that—and Catherine always felt somehow more vibrant and interesting because of it. "How are you?"

"Wondering if you're still taking in visitors from the old country?"

"Depends on the visitor," May replied playfully.

"Me," said Catherine—then had to pull the phone abruptly from her ear as May squealed at the other end.

"I thought you were *never* going to come!" May managed finally, when she'd calmed down.

"I thought so too."

"When were you thinking?"

"As soon as convenient for Stanley and you."

There was much excited chatter—they were on the phone for nearly an hour as May talked excitedly about all the things they could do, the people she wanted her to meet, and the places on the island she wanted to show her.

By the end of the call they'd agreed she was to visit in a month's time.

The following morning, Catherine spent a cathartic few hours going through her wardrobe. Ruthlessly purging almost everything in the third cupboard, along with a good deal from the second, her selection criterion was very simple: if she didn't feel great in it, she was throwing it out. No longer would she deny herself her best clothes or favorite outfits. No longer was she going to make do, or put up with the dated, the dull or the second best. She had a cupboard full of beautiful clothes and she was going to wear them!

Saturday afternoon was spent applying much the same principle to her crockery cabinets. Out went the "everyday" service, which she'd routinely used for the past twenty years. Neatly wrapping and stacking the plates and bowls into cardboard packing boxes, she replaced the items with the much loved but almost never used porcelain given to Klaus and her as a wedding gift by his parents. She emptied the cutlery drawers and refilled them with the silver dinner service. And she switched her most treasured glassware from the rarely used dining room to the kitchen. For as many, or as few, glasses of water or wine she had left to drink on this earth, she resolved, she would do so using the generous, beautifully shaped glasses that gave her such pleasure.

That night, with unusual spontaneity, she invited both sons and their families round to eat takeaway meals off the best family china, and to quaff champagne from the many cases that Klaus had stored downstairs. Her sons and daughter-in-laws were more than curious about what had brought about the unexpected changes. She told them that it was really quite simple: working in the City Morgue had made her realize she wouldn't live forever. She may as well make the most of each single day that she had the incomprehensible good fortune of waking up to.

She could tell, by their expressions, that they didn't really get it. That their own death was still an intellectual abstraction. Something around the corner. Over the horizon. Like her own had been until she'd worked at the City Morgue. Just as she knew that no amount of talk could help them reach the same realization that she had. *That* was a recognition that went deeper than words.

She spent a lot of time over the next week ferrying unwanted clothes and housewares to local charity shops. Carefully choosing which bundle of items should go to which not-for-profit, each of the deliveries was accompanied by a note carefully handwritten on quality Venetian notepaper, sometimes embossed or illustrated, and in each case written upon with heartfelt gratitude.

Catherine had written and posted another important missive, the response to which came to occupy her thoughts each day after she had slipped it into the mailbox near her home. She had thought very carefully about the words she had written, expressing herself in a way that was as deliberately neutral and open as possible.

Fortunately, she didn't have long to wait for a response. Late that same week the phone rang one evening shortly after 8 pm. It was her brother Gerry. He'd got her note, he said. He was pleased she'd made contact. During the long conversation that followed, there wasn't a thing he said that surprised her as he recounted his former wife's inexplicable resentment of the family, or his own, conflicted feelings when he finally got a divorce.

What did surprise her, however, was the way just listening to his voice made her feel. A voice she hadn't heard for well over ten years and yet which she knew so very well. It came as an unexpected and joyful reminder of how wonderful it felt to have a brother again.

In no time at all, Catherine was on her way to the Bahamas, where she was immediately caught up in the social vortex of May's life, and introduced as "Katie" to May and Stanley's friends. There was the welcoming party at their home on her very first weekend. The yacht club regatta. The art exhibition and informal socializing that seemed to accompany even the most mundane trip to the local shops.

It was at social tennis on her first Sunday that she met May's photographer friend Ant—and felt an instant connection. Ant evidently felt it too. He had soon offered her a tour of his favorite island scenery, and, re-experiencing the same intensity of feelings she had as a young girl asked out on a date, she had said yes.

During the days that followed, one thing led inevitably to the other. May was not only aware of the blossoming romance, but actively encouraging it. And although Catherine felt deeply insecure about revealing her body to a man who wasn't her husband—the first time such a thing would have happened in thirty years—to the point that, before, she would have stopped things well before they could get that far—with Ant she felt different.

Nature took its course, and far from feeling inhibited and undesirable, Katie relished their intimacy. Making love was different from the way it had been in the past. But she was thrilled by the rapture, the ecstatic connection she had long-since assumed to be a thing of the past.

Katie didn't know where things with Ant were going. But nor did she think much about it. They were here, now, unreserved in their adoration of one another and in making the most of each, precious moment.

"I sometimes wonder if these aren't the best days of our lives," Ant said, one morning, as they sat on the balcony outside his bedroom, looking across the palm-tops towards the sea.

"If you have the good fortune to reach our age with some level of financial independence, and the kids are making their own way in the world and you're in good health, has there ever been a better time to be alive?"

Reaching out, Katie had squeezed his hand. "Not for me," she said.

When Katie Turner looked in the mirror, she felt more vibrant and alive than she had for many years. The 52-year-old woman returning her gaze had a holiday tan and a sparkle in her eye. Stepping back from the mirror no longer bothered her. Nor was she startled by unexpected glimpses of herself in shop windows. She was alive, was she not? Gloriously, wonderfully alive! The possessor of robust health and happiness. Someone with the immense good fortune to share her life and love with others.

How to deal with the rush of thoughts and feelings that bubbled up to the surface at such moments? For Katie there was a phrase that summed it up. "Heartfelt gratitude" was her chosen philosophy. Heartfelt gratitude for the fact that every day she woke up was the most precious of gifts, one never to be taken for granted, especially given her deeply held conviction that there had never been a better time to be alive.

A CHANGE OF HEART

"Tell me, where is fancy bred,
in the heart or in the head?'
Shakespeare, *The Merchant of Venice*, Act 3, Scene 1

A HAM AND CHEESE SANDWICH, UNEATEN, WAS THE FIRST SIGN THAT change was afoot in the life of Ken Kroaker. But it was a sign so subtle given the enormity of what had just happened, and its implications so easily missed, that no one picked up on it at the time.

Not even the patient himself.

The sandwich was lying on the bone china plate of his private hospital ward when a nurse came in to check on him.

"Not up to lunch?" she asked sympathetically, her gaze sweeping the monitors of the range of machines to which he was hooked up.

The fifty-eight-year-old man shook his head. After a full day on ventilation, and with an encyclopedia of drugs pumping through his system—pain management, anti-infective, anti-rejection to name only a few—Ken Kroaker wasn't looking his best. Deep, midnight shadows had formed under his eyes. His face was smudged with two days of unshaven stubble. His hair, graying and disheveled, stuck out at wild angles from his head. He certainly looked nothing like the domineering tycoon portrayed on the glossy front cover of *Business Today* only three weeks before.

But for a man who had just gone through major surgery, he wasn't in bad shape either.

"Don't feel like ham," he said.

The nurse tilted her chin. "Could we tempt you with another filling?"

"Just cheese," he said.

"I'll see to it." She removed the tray from his side table and moved towards the door. "The sooner we have you eating and drinking for yourself, the better."

The call from the hospital had come at an especially bad time. Months before, he had put into action events that were planned to culminate in the biggest business deal of his life, a deal he might be called upon, at any moment, to act upon. A deal that would not only make Kroaker Construction by far the biggest builder in the city, but that had the potential to wipe his competitors clean off the map. It was a deal that had become his obsession, working from his eyrie on the 40th floor of Kroaker Tower, one of the tallest buildings in the city, on which his name was emblazoned in scarlet, neon letters.

But when you have suffered from repeated heart failure and you've made it to the transplant waiting list and suddenly, out of nowhere, you're told that a compatible organ has become available, there is only one answer.

The cardiac surgeon had called him last Wednesday evening at 8 pm. By 9:30 pm he was in hospital preparing to have his sternum sawed open.

One and a half days later, and thanks to the advances of medical technology, he was munching on a cheese sandwich when his wife and sons came to visit.

"Darling!" Barbara strode in. The second Mrs. Kroaker was, every inch of her, the fashion model she had once been, tall, poised, her blonde hair falling in an elegant curtain to her shoulders. As she leaned to kiss him, he was engulfed in a familiar cloud of her favorite perfume, and he found himself thinking how very beauti-ful it was. She was. This unfamiliar thought prompted an equally unfamiliar feeling, so when she slipped her hand into his, he felt an entirely uncharacteristic welling up of emotion.

Behind her trooped the two boys, both in the dark suits he required them to wear to the office. Aidan, at twenty-six, only twelve years younger than Barbara, looked the part of the man about town, as he always did with his dark, slicked back hair, expensive suit and confident demeanor. Troy, two years his junior, was wearing his usual, goofy, grin. As the boys lined up at the foot of his bed, an unfamiliar milieu for them all, the feeling in the room was as if they had been summoned to the headmaster's office.

"Dad!" Aidan greeted him with a firm nod of the chin.

"All good?" inquired Troy.

Ken reacted to his second son almost from instinct, looking down with silent deliberation at the dozen lines running out of his body to the array of bleeping equipment alongside him.

Picking up on the unspoken admonition, Barbara was quick to move things along. "Mr. White was very pleased with the procedure," she said, referring to his cardiac surgeon. "Said it went as smoothly as these things can."

Aidan nodded encouragingly. "On track to go home within 10 days," he said.

"Home." Barbara countered immediately. "Not the office."

She knew nothing of the deal her husband had been planning, but she knew that there was one, and that Aidan was in on it. The two of them had been as thick as thieves.

"Of course." Aidan leveled his father with a gaze that was defiantly void of any meaning.

Ken glanced from Aidan's vacant stare, to his wife whose lips were formed in a tight smile, to Troy, staring out the window to the football field next to the hospital. And he felt strange. Disoriented. His first, post-operative encounter with the immediate family was exactly as he would have expected. But in a different way he found it hard to identify, something seemed to be awry.

His eyelids blinked heavily shut. "Tired," he said.

"You must get your rest." He felt Barbara lean to kiss him on the forehead.

The boys chimed their goodbyes.

"We'll come to visit tomorrow" said Barbara.

"Hmph."

They did visit him the next day. And the day after that. Barbara was nothing if not dutiful. She'd always arrive immaculate and fragrant, bearing flowers and favorite treats to make his stay more tolerable. Sometimes one or both of the boys would be with her. And each day Ken was a little more robust. More alert and focused on what was happening around him.

But the sensation that something was amiss didn't go away. If anything, it got only stronger.

The visit he had really wanted came a week after his operation. At 9:30 on a Wednesday morning, Aidan arrived with Ben Riddell in tow. Riddell was head of security at Kroaker, a job that notionally put him in charge of protecting the various premises and construction sites the company owned across the city. But the reason he had hired a former high-level intelligence officer for one of the highest paid roles in his company had nothing to do with his ability to roster guards or manage CCTV cameras.

"Are you well enough for a briefing?" Riddell had asked.

He'd nodded. He was no longer intubated in any way. He was showering and using the bathroom without the need to summon help. Shaving that morning, he had noticed that a faint glow had returned to his cheeks.

Just like he'd noticed that other weird thing. As he'd smoothed shaving cream onto his face, the word "tender" had come into his head. And kept repeating all the while he was shaving. "Tender, tender, tender!" It kept going around and around in his mind, driving him crazy. What was all that about?

Now he looked at Riddell, a man with an instantly forgettable face, wearing corporate clothes that made no statement one way or another, and who spoke in an even voice. "Everything is going to plan," he said.

Kroaker nodded.

"The pips are starting to squeak."

The plan he was referring to was one that had evolved at The Construction Association Awards Banquet 15 months earlier. Or, at least, Kroaker had made it seem that way. While there were hundreds of construction firms and thousands of subcontractors in the city, only four developers dominated the market, of which Kroaker was one.

Tony Manolos, whose name appeared in blue neon letters on top of the skyscraper up the street from Kroaker Tower, and Pieter Parker, based in the industrial area, were, like him, old school operators who'd pulled themselves up by their own bootstraps, having started out as one-man bands decades earlier. Phil Faber was a professional CEO who'd been parachuted in to run the local operations of a national construction firm. Over the decades, as they'd competed in the market, they had constantly clashed in their bids to win lucrative contracts, grab new land subdivisions and fight for market share.

As their companies engaged in relentless and brutal warfare, on a personal basis the four men were self-consciously civil to one another on the rare occasions they met. It was as if any signal of being affronted gave the other man the upper hand.

At last year's banquet, they had found themselves in a room next to the Grand Ballroom, being photographed for a profile piece on The Big Four.

"Should be the Big Five," Kroaker had planted the seed, as they stood, looking misleadingly collegiate, beaming for the camera.

"You mean Tarsich?" Manolos had always been sharp as a nail gun.

"He's made more money than any of us," confirmed Kroaker.

If there was one name universally reviled in the construction industry, it was that of Tyrone Tarsich. Owner of Tarsich Brickworks, he had a monopoly. And because the city was so far from anywhere else, and the cost of setting up in competition to Tarsich was prohibitive, Tarsich had been able to charge whatever he liked for his bricks. Which hadn't been a problem in times gone by. But in recent years, things had been getting out of hand.

"And he's made it out of us." Pieter Parker never shied away from stating the obvious.

"Eight percent increases two years in a row," said Faber.

"It's hurting *our* bottom line," Kroaker allowed for scripted vulnerability, knowing full well it was the same for all of them. "Rumor has it, he's sledging us with a similar hike this year."

"Someone's got to stop him," said Manolos, obligingly.

Kroaker allowed time for this to sink in before offering, "There's only four people who can."

After the photo session, they closed in around him, wanting to know what he meant, exactly. "There's hundreds of builders in this town, but the four of us account for, what, eighty percent of his sales?"

"There's nowhere else to go," said Pieter Parker.

"He's doing nothing illegal," said Tony Manolos.

"We can't join forces or he'll slap us with a lawsuit," said Phil Faber.

Kroaker paused before making his apparently spontaneous suggestion. "But all four of us can stockpile more bricks than we need. Say, for a year."

There were blank expressions, before the light bulb went on in Manolos's eyes, "Then stop ordering?"

"Exactly."

"For months," confirmed Manolos.

Pieter Parker grinned. "Let's see him going without an order from any of us for six months."

"He'd become a lot more … customer focused," observed Phil Faber with elaborate understatement.

Sure enough, Tyrone Tarsich had put up the price of bricks by 8 percent a couple of months later. And, to his surprise, he found the response of his major customers was to step up their orders. So much so, he was forced to take out a bank loan to expand his plant to keep up with demand.

Now, however, it was month two of the mind-focusing period the Big Four had worked out among themselves. Not a single order had gone into Tarsich Bricks from any of them for over seven weeks. And the pips, as Riddell had put it, were indeed starting to squeak.

"He called in his Sales Director on Monday," Riddell reported now. "These past few weeks he's been using the "lumpy ordering" argument. They're starting to twig that it's more than that. They've had to shut down output fifty percent. They've a yard so full of bricks there's no space left. And they're hemorrhaging cash to pay for the expanded capacity they're not using."

Aidan pumped a fist into his open palm with glee.

"And the other builders?" asked Kroaker.

"Sticking to the agreed line. Non-committal about when their next order will be."

The strategy the Big Four had agreed was to say nothing to Tarsich, nor to put in any orders for three months. Let him sweat it out. Then they'd go in and have the conversation. They'd propose a 50 percent price cut as a low-ball opener, with a view to accepting nothing less than 30 percent. All four companies had enough bricks to last six months. They could hold out till Tarsich had to come to the table.

Kroaker leaned against his hospital pillow taking it all in. Remembering the game plan he'd so meticulously put in place. It was rare in an industry, with so much ingrained enmity, to get competitors to work together, but that was exactly what was happening. Or seemed to be. Because what Manolos, Parker and Faber didn't know was that they were playing directly into his hands.

Kroaker's secret weapon was Riddell, a man whose surveillance methods were those he'd learned working in global espionage. Hence, Kroaker knew that Tyrone Tarsich was an ill man, with slow-growing but terminal cancer, exacerbated by stress. A man who, unlike Kroaker, had no sons or succession plan. A man who was coming round to his wife's strongly-held view that he should sell the business and live a full and stress-free life for as long as he was able.

Kroaker was waiting for Riddell to give him the signal that it was the very best moment for him to have a very different conversation with Tarsich, ideally in Mrs. Tarsich's presence. One that went along the lines: it's all getting too hard for the brickworks. I'll take the business off your hands. But I need an answer now.

Even if he ended up paying top dollar, it would be worth it. As soon as Kroaker controlled Tarsich Bricks, he controlled his competitors. *He* would set the price of their bricks, while getting his own at cost. While their input costs steadily climbed, his own would fall. Project by project he'd undercut them so that they'd lose business, shed staff, become shadows of their former selves. One day perhaps, after clearing out all their senior staff, he'd reduce them to mere divisions of Kroaker Construction.

"Your being here hasn't been a problem at all, Dad," Aidan confirmed now. "Things are working out fine. And you'll be … available again from Friday."

What his son said was true. As soon as Riddell indicated that Tarsich was vulnerable, he was in a position to swoop. Which made the sudden and overwhelming feeling of nausea that surged up inside him all the more inexplicable—and unfortunate. Lurching off his bed, he hurried to the private bathroom.

"Have to—"

"We'll keep you briefed." Riddell and Aidan scurried off.

Kroaker was on his knees in the bathroom, nauseous but unable to vomit. Clammy and shivering, as he crouched over the toilet bowl, forehead resting on his hands, for a long while the only thing he was aware of was the sensation of his new heart, pounding.

Lub dub, lub dub, lub dub.

And, from out of nowhere, that crazy chant that had run through his mind this morning as he was shaving: tender, tender, tender!

Tender, tender, tender!

He told the nurse he wanted to see the cardiologist. *Before* Barbara's planned visit at four. Certain things needed to be asked that he'd feel self-conscious querying in front of her.

"Any questions?" asked Mr. White, having checked his vital statistics, and found them to be satisfactory.

"I've been having these … weird feelings," he said.

"How do you mean?"

How to find the words to explain something he didn't understand himself? Something he'd picked up on the very first time Barbara and the boys had visited, but that didn't, necessarily, have anything to do with them. That same, inexplicable sensation had been even more acute when Riddell had given his briefing.

"Things don't seem right," was the only way he could account for it.

"Your vision is normal?"

"Fine."

"Hearing."

"No change."

"What about taste?"

"I like bacon. But not this morning. Took one look at the cooked breakfast and it made me sick. Like the lamb last night."

Mr. White was nodding. "Very typical. Your balance will be out of whack for a time."

"I keep getting these … strange ideas." He glanced towards the door.

"Oh?"

"Like African music. Suddenly, I just want to listen to it. I had my wife download some for me yesterday."

White smiled indulgently. "Listening to music isn't injurious to your health. Exploring new genres may help you pass the time more pleasantly."

"I've had some pretty weird dreams."

"Your body has been through serious trauma."

"A couple of times my wife has been in and I've had these strong … emotions."

"Ken." The doctor reached out and squeezed his hand briefly. "You have just survived major surgery. An operation that, as I counseled you, is not without risk. You wouldn't be human if that hadn't stirred up all kinds of feelings."

"So, all the strange things. Being revolted by meat. Wanting African music. That's nothing to do with the new heart?"

"The heart is a pump. One hell of a pump. But that's all. You're on very high doses of anti-rejection drugs. These inevitably have an impact on your affective state."

Kroaker watched the cardiologist leave his room a few minutes later. As he did, it was with the curious sensation that the pre-op Ken Kroaker would have accepted the doctor's explanation about what was happening, and left it at that.

But Ken Kroaker 2.0 had the sense that there was more to it. Things, in a profound way that he couldn't express, just weren't making sense.

Each day that passed, was a day closer to being able to leave. A day out of the red zone when he wouldn't be available to clinch the long-planned, and greatly anticipated deal.

Finally the moment of his release came, and the first thing he wanted to do was get a haircut. He'd been in need of one when he got the call for the new heart. That had been ten days before.

"Shall I make an appointment at Devlin's?" Barbara had offered, when they'd been planning his return home.

He'd been a client of Devlin's Gentleman's Hair Lounge for years—not only for the haircuts, but also for the corporate tittle-tattle that Charles Devlin shared with his more influential patrons.

Kroaker shook his head. "I'll go somewhere more casual," he'd said.

To Barbara's surprise, as she sat behind the steering wheel of the Phantom, he directed her into Westbridge, one of those grungy suburbs you find near the central train station of most cities, containing streets lined with alternative food stores, Adult XXX shops, and the boarded up former offices of Marxist protest groups. She was amazed he even knew about the existence of the tiny barber's store, sandwiched between an Asian takeaway and a run-down snooker hall.

She was even more amazed when he emerged from it, twenty minutes later with no hair at all. His bald pate gleamed in the afternoon sun as he crossed the pavement to where she was waiting for him in the car.

"Decided to take it all off," he told her, unnecessarily, slipping into the passenger seat.

Barbara was at a loss for words. The haircut was abruptly and dramatically out of character. She fixed him with a quizzical smile. "It's a surprise," she said.

"Surprised myself."

"I wouldn't have thought you'd know this part of the world," she said, pulling into the afternoon traffic.

"Don't." He shrugged. "I just had a feeling there would be a barber shop here. Kind of weird."

As if to reinforce what he'd just said, as he put his hand up to feel the unfamiliar smoothness of his completely shaven head, the "tender" chant started up again in his head. If anything, it seemed even more insistent than before.

Barbara had wanted a "Welcome Home" family dinner. On previous celebratory occasions, they had asked their chef, headhunted from one of the city's top restaurants, to prepare a meal of considerable gastronomic ingenuity. Not this time. Ken asked for a casual, vegetarian buffet lunch.

"I seem to have gone off meat," he announced to the family. Which, in the Kroaker household meant that they had gone off meat too.

For Kroaker, the lunch was a continuation of his post-transplant surreality. Opposite where he and Barbara sat together at the terrace table, Aidan outlined his plans for the 60 meter super yacht he would be commissioning, as soon as the Tarsich Brick deal was bedded down, and he was running the building firm, while his brother ran the brickworks—the plan his father had set in motion.

Next to him, his fiancé Jemima, a diamond-encrusted 24 year old with a brittle laugh, complained bitterly about being let down by their interior designer, who had apparently arrived bearing parrot print cushion covers for the pool house of their new mansion—completely out of keeping with the prescribed Grecian theme.

Troy sat on the same side as the table as Ken, using Barbara as a shield from his father. He had spent all morning drinking beer and was as monosyllabic as ever. The only subject on which he spoke with interest was South American football teams, a subject on which he was expert.

Ken sat there, taking it all in, and couldn't avoid the powerful feelings of entitlement, premature middle-agedness and sheer banality in his family. How could he have possibly missed it before?

That evening they went upstairs to bed early. Ken heard Barbara in the shower and, a short while later, through the half-opened door of the bathroom, saw her reflected in the mirror as she stepped onto a bathmat. Watching her towel herself dry he became aroused.

A few moments later, he had stripped off, and appeared behind her in the mirror, as she brushed her blonde mane. Resting his chin on her shoulder, he put his arms around her waist.

"You're a very attractive woman, Barbs," he said, his hands roving upwards, his meaning unmistakable.

How could he put into words what was going on in his mind? His body? They had been together for seven years, but in the strangest of ways he felt as if he was seeing her, naked, for the first time. And he was a young man again.

Barbara reached behind with her hand and grasped where he was already standing to full attention.

"Oh!" She met his eyes in the mirror with a look of playfulness. "Unexpected?"

"I know."

She turned round so that they were face to face. "Interesting what a new heart and ten days in hospital can do."

"Everything's feeling, well, the same, but also different."

"I know," she said, placing both hands on his newly bald head and sliding them down his cheeks as she fixed him with a knowing look, "Well, it looks like I'm on top. We can't have you straining your sternum."

She used the phrase Mr. White had warned them about emphatically during his sermon on post-operative care.

The following day, Ken called a number in one of the brochures the cardiologist had given him. It was a heart transplant patients' support group. At the time that Mr. White had handed over the sheaf of documents, pre-op, Kroaker hadn't thought, for one single moment, that he would be calling on the help of what he'd instantly categorized as a bunch of namby-pamby, do-gooders pandering to the whims of the feeble-minded.

But that was before he'd gone vegetarian. And shaven his head. And discovered a passion for the African marimba.

"I recently had a transplant, and am looking for some answers," he began, relieved when he was asked only for a first name.

"That's why we're here."

"I've been experiencing changes since the operation."

"Oh yes," the man at the other end responded smoothly. "Like different dietary preferences?"

"Yes. Exactly."

"Unexpected likes and dislikes?"

"Yes."

"Perceiving things and people differently?"

"Is this common?"

"And the doctors are telling you it's all about the anti-rejection drugs?"

The guy seemed clairvoyant!

"The medical world doesn't like talking about the non-physiological impact of heart transplants."

"Why not?"

"Because they can't explain it.'The other sighed. "Or rather, explaining it just opens up a Pandora's Box and they don't want to go there. Which is okay for them. They're not the ones with the new heart."

They arranged to meet at a coffee shop, a branch of one of those anonymous chains where everything is reassuringly similar in the blandest possible way. Ken was supposed to be taking it easy at home, but summoned a corporate vehicle while Barbara was doing roll-downs at Pilates.

It so happened that Greg, the man who had taken his call, had been the recipient of a new heart three years earlier. A police detective by training, he had made it his mission to research why he had developed an unprecedented craving for alcopops and shooter drinks.

"The heart is the most energetic organ in the body," he told Ken, after they were sitting opposite one another, sharing a pot of chamomile tea. "It beats one hundred thousand times a day. Clinicians like to talk about it as though it's only a pump. But it's a lot more than that. Problem is, they haven't worked out a theory to explain what's going on."

Ken regarded the tall, skinny man opposite with a querying look. "And you have?"

"Not me personally." He shrugged. "But as heart transplants become more common, and there's more people like you and me with these experiences, well, the evidence is building. We're getting to a point where it can no longer be waved away as the side effects of anti-rejection drugs."

"So what's your take?"

"At the most basic level, when someone else's heart is put in your chest, you're not just getting a new pump. You're getting elements, influences—call it what you like—of their personality."

Kroaker raised his eyebrows. In a way it sounded strange to hear it said out loud like that. In a different way, his thoughts had been moving along much the same lines.

"What you're saying—" he cut to the chase "—is that the heart somehow contains memories? Likes and dislikes?"

"That's the materialist model," the other nodded. "Called cellular memory. Problem is, despite billions of dollars in research, scientists have yet to show how any cells can store memories. And what happens to the contained memories when the cells die, which they are doing continuously? How does one cell pass memories onto its replacement?"

Kroaker leaned back in his seat. They were getting into deep waters. He had never given a moment's thought to the mechanism by which people remembered things. But the way this guy described it, cellular memory seemed unlikely.

"There's another explanation?" he wanted to know.

"More radical, in a way, but also more traditional," Greg smiled. "The other model sees the heart as the energetic center of the body, the conductor of the whole performance so to speak. When we take it out of somebody it still bears an imprint of their consciousness."

"So we're affected by them when we get a transplant?"

"Exactly. Their likes and dislikes. Alcopops and shooters. Powerful memories. Even their connections to others."

Kroaker cocked his chin. He hadn't experienced unaccountable feelings of being connected to people in the few days since the operation. But the very idea of it was new and quite disturbing. "You can be … affected by people you don't even know?" he asked, eyebrows raised.

"At a heart level," Greg finished for him. "For reasons that make no sense at all. Unless you understand the consciousness model."

On his way home from the meeting, they stopped at a bookstore so he could pick up a few titles that Greg had recommended. Kroaker hadn't read a book in years. But he was soon poring over shelves labeled Esoteric Traditions, Mind-Body Science and Quantum Physics with an enthusiasm that combined powerful feelings of intense curiosity with deep familiarity.

As they arrived back home, the driver pressed the buzzer to announce himself to security, who operated the gate. They slowly proceeded up the driveway, past where the gardening team was busy tending to the lawn terraces and landscaped flower beds. Coming to a halt under the portico, the butler had already appeared at the front door, to help him up the few steps inside. Pausing for a moment at the entrance to the Palladian mansion, taking it all in, his admiration for the immaculate magnificence and industry he saw all around him was joined by a startling, new feeling: how utterly pointless it all seemed.

He helped himself to some snacks from the fridge, much to Chef's horror, including a packet of vegetables and a tub of hummus. He had been planning to settle into an armchair in his office to go through the books he had just bought. But all the photographs of flagship Kroaker Construction buildings, the architectural diagrams, and industry awards felt somehow oppressive. Instead he made his way to their bedroom, which had a lighter and airier feel. Deciding to change out of the clothes he'd worn to the meeting, his gaze just happened to rest on Barbara's collection of bathrobes. The orange one in particular.

When Barbara returned home from Pilates, it was to discover her shaved-headed, orange-robed husband sprawled on the sofa, while African music piped in the background, devouring a book about the convergence of quantum science and Eastern mind training, with evident enthusiasm.

"This is amazing!" He waved the book at her from the sofa. "All these years I've been a materialist, without realizing that matter and energy are different aspects of the same reality."

In yoga pants, her blonde hair pulled back in a ponytail, Barbara was slightly flushed after her exertions, but poised and graceful as ever. Quite used to conversational ambushes from her self-involved husband, what was different about this one was the subject matter: not a stock pick or commercial deal, but the nature of reality.

"I s'pose that makes sense," she said.

"Glad you agree." He waved a packet of vegetable crudités in her direction. "Carrot?"

In the days that followed, Ken Kroaker grew steadily stronger. And he spent a lot of time pursuing his new interests, reading books, watching YouTube videos and downloading files from all manner of websites. Under strict instructions not to return to the office for at least three weeks, Barbara was surprised how compliant he was with doctors' orders. Although it didn't escape her that this appeared more a result of a growing disinterest in business, rather than out of self-discipline.

Aidan would stop by the house daily, with the latest news on Tarsich. In the past, her husband would have wanted to know about every conversation, every shift of circumstances on the front line. Aidan would gloatingly report about the collapse in output at the brickworks. How Tarsich had been forced to lease an old quarry for storage. As each day went by, events seemed to be moving towards the demise of Tarsich Bricks with mounting inevitability.

Instead of reveling in every detail, as he would have in the past, Ken Kroaker was more distant. "Until Riddell gives us the green light, it's all hypothetical," he kept on saying.

Nevertheless, he wasn't completely inactive on the work front. He had given considerable thought to the plan to pull the rug from under the feet of his competitors, and make Tarsich Bricks his own. He had imagined their reaction to hearing the news. The impact it would have on their businesses and staff. In particular, for reasons Kroaker couldn't account for, he kept coming back to Tony Manolos, who presided over the high-rise building with the blue neon sign up the street from Kroaker HQ.

Of all his competitors, Manolos was the smartest. The moment he heard what had happened, he would see the writing on the wall—and adapt. He'd summon his most senior staff and the redundancies would begin. It would be a bloodbath in there.

Going online, Kroaker found himself navigating through the Manolos website, studying photographs of his Directors and Senior Management Team. It was at that particular moment that he began to feel physically sick. Pushing back from his desk, the queasy feeling evolved rapidly into a more visceral biliousness. He hurried to the toilet and found himself down again on all fours, disorientated and perspiring, waiting for the violent heave through his body that never came. And all the while he was there, forehead resting on the porcelain bowl, the throbbing of his new heart seemed to resonate throughout his whole body: *lub dub, lub dub, lub dub.*

Along with the crazy, repetitive syllables: "Tender, tender, tender, tender!"

One night Barbara woke up in the early hours to discover he was no longer in their bed, or bathroom. In fact, nowhere to be found in the house.

He was downstairs walking across the lawn barefoot, in her orange bathroom.

"Are you alright, darling?" she called softly, as she approached. She wondered if he was sleepwalking.

"I feel like I'm only starting to wake up, from being asleep my whole life," he told her, speaking in a tone that, far from being somnambulant, was lucidly clear. "I have all this money, and the power that it buys, but I don't do anything useful with it besides make more money, and acquire more power, because that's all that I know how to do. Only, it's completely without purpose. I realize that now.

"When my consciousness moves out of this body, like my donor's moved out of his, I can't take the money, the properties, the cars. I can only go with the way I am. Or, at least, the way I have become. In my case, a self-centered control freak who doesn't give a damn how many people's lives he wrecks for an extra buck."

"Darling—"

"It's true! I can see it now with sobering clarity. Just like that Shantideva guy says," he quoted from one of the books he had been reading:

""*Although wishing to be rid of misery,*
They rush towards misery itself.
Although wishing to have happiness,
Like an enemy they ignorantly destroy it."

"Do you know, it's taken me until now to realize I don't even know what wellbeing actually feels like? It's only now I've been able to see that the only thing that really matters in life is whether we move towards love and light, or towards self-interest and darkness."

"It's not too late to change."

He turned to her. "But how would you cope, being married to a different person?"

"You already are different." Her tone was gentle.

He nodded.

"And I like the differentness."

"Really?"

"Not the part that involves stealing my bathrobes." She smiled. "But the other parts."

He slipped his arm around her.

"To be honest, I was getting so fed up with the old Ken Kroaker, I was beginning to wonder how long we could last."

The call finally came from Riddell. "He had a doctor's appointment this morning, where they reviewed last week's tests," Riddell told him.

Kroaker had never asked Riddell how, exactly, he came by all his intelligence. It was something he preferred not to know.

"His blood count is terrible. His wife knows he's battling major problems at work. She's practically demanded that he quit, to take care of himself. The time is perfect."

Like other Big Four bosses, Kroaker had had dealings with Tyrone Tarsich over the years. They had been businesslike. Confrontational. Unlike Pieter Parker, he had resisted throwing a marble ashtray at him. He hadn't spoken to Tarsich for years, but given the absence of orders from all four of the majors, he reckoned the brick boss would be willing to see him at short notice.

He wasn't wrong. Within five minutes of asking his personal assistant to set up a meeting asap, she had phoned him back with a time for that afternoon.

With the appointment fixed, Kroaker closed the door of his home office, and made a few calls.

Both Aidan and Troy were waiting for him, back at the house, when Kroaker returned from High Noon. It was nearly seven in the evening—the meeting had gone on for two hours.

"How did it go?" Aidan wanted to know the moment he stepped through the front door.

He nodded. "Good meeting."

"Do we have a deal?"

"Settle down and fix me a chamomile tea," he said. "Time for a family meeting in the garden."

"The garden?!"

"Perfect evening to sit on the grass."

It was a balmy evening, and fragrances of a multitude of blossoms wafted over from the flower beds.

Behind Kroaker's back, Aidan exchanged a glance with Troy, twirling his finger beside his ear in a gesture suggesting insanity.

When all four of them were seated on the grass a short while later, Kroaker turned to his sons.

"In the past couple of weeks since my operation, I've had a lot of time to think about things," he began. "As your father, I feel that I have let you down. Forced you into jobs and situations you wouldn't have chosen for yourself. To lead lives that aren't authentic. Troy, you'd be much happier getting a job doing something in football.

Troy acknowledged this with a lopsided smile.

"And I apologize for my bullying ways and compulsion to belittle you. It's like I haven't been able to help myself. But I promise I will try much harder to be a better man. A more ... loving father."

Putting his arms around his knees and lowering his head, Troy couldn't suppress an involuntary heave of emotion. Next to him, Barbara reached out to give him a hug.

"Aidan," Kroaker continued, "you need to spread your wings, try out new things, live a little. There's plenty of time to marry and settle down later."

"But Jemima ... loves me."

"She loves your money," he retorted. "My money. Which she hopes will become hers."

Aidan scowled. "What about the Tarsich deal?"

"I've done something different."

"You've what?"

"The Tarsich deal would have delivered more influence and, in time, money. But what for? We already have much more money than we need."

"How is that even possible?" Aidan demanded, angrily. "Compared to the Omni family, we're nothing!"

"Right now you can smell the fragrance of night jasmine, coming from the trellis over there." Kroaker gestured to a paved area under a white trellis in which bowers of jasmine had burst into prolific bloom. "Do you know how many times I've sat and enjoyed that scent in the ten years we've lived here? Maybe twice. It's not money that we're short of. It's time!"

"What've you done about Tarsich?!" Aidan's voice rose in anger.

"He's selling to The Construction Association."

"You're crazy!" No longer able to contain his fury, Aidan leapt to his feet.

"Seems fair to me. This way, all the builders pay a fair price."

"But you could have taken the lot."

"How would that have benefited the industry? The people of our city?"

"What have *they* got to do with it?" Aidan spat.

"Just so you know, I've also agreed to sell Kroaker to Federal Construction."

"Sell?" It was Barbara who gave voice to their mutual surprise."

"Federal wants a footprint in our city. They've been courting me for months. I've decided to cash out and set up a charitable foundation. Play Santa for the rest of our lives." He squeezed Barbara's hand.

"Where does that leave me?" demanded Aidan.

"With a new boss," Kroaker replied evenly. "Unless you'd rather do something else. This is your chance for a fresh start too."

The meeting didn't happen until nearly a full year later. Kroaker wasn't given the names of the parents. He was only asked to nominate somewhere to meet that was neutral territory. For no particular reason, he suggested Wild Ginger, a vegetarian café in Westbridge, on the last Friday of that month.

The transplant service had needed to go through protocols, to get permissions, to allow grieving time for the mother and father of the young man whose heart now beat inside him. They had also sent a counselor round to make sure he and Barbara were emotionally ready. They suggested they prepare a list of questions they may like to ask.

For Ken Kroaker that was easy. There was only one thing he wanted to know, and he was reminded of it so very frequently that he had absolutely no need to write it down: where in God's name did "*Tender, tender, tender, tender*" come from? Why did it come into his mind so frequently, at different times of the day and night?

He sat with his back to the door, Barbara facing out. He was curiously, unfamiliarly nervous.

The meeting wasn't due till eleven. But at ten to he told Barbara, "They're very close," he touched his heart. "I know."

He remembered being told by Greg, the volunteer guy, about sensing connections. But in the twelve months since the transplant, this was the first time he'd actually felt it.

At five to eleven, he looked into his wife's eyes. "They're here."

She glanced up to where a couple in their fifties were opening the café door.

When Kroaker got up and turned, both he and the father were in for the surprise of their lives.

"Ken Kroaker!" Manolos's right-hand man moved towards him, anticipation mixed with incredulity.

"Steve!" Kroaker reached out to shake his hand before, thinking better of it, embraced him briefly.

They sat, the astonishment of their mutual recognition followed by stunned silence.

Christine Hartley was the first to recover. A well put together woman in her forties, she asked Kroaker, "How did you know about this place?"

Kroaker was puzzled, "Know?"

"It was Will's favorite."

"Your son?" he confirmed.

They nodded.

"I didn't know. I mean, I've been here a couple of times. Felt kind of …drawn to it. Your son has turned me into a vegetarian."

The Hartleys looked startled.

"It's true," confirmed Barbara. "He hasn't touched meat since the transplant. The new heart has affected him in more ways than you can imagine."

Kroaker looked from Steve to Christine before saying after a while, "And African music. Can't get enough of it."

Christine put her hands to her mouth. "He loved it!" She was nodding, "That's why we're here, right? Today?"

Again, lines appeared on Ken Kroaker's forehead. "How do you mean, today?"

"You really didn't know?" Steve pointed to a poster on a wall, which the Kroakers had missed. The headline announced a fundraiser on the last Friday of every month for an African charity in the community hall next door. The poster featured an exuberant group playing African marimbas, or xylophones.

"Will was a big supporter of them," said Steve.

"I sometimes came with him," said Christine. "He was always so happy to be here." Her eyes glistened.

"And tell me," said Kroaker. "Was he also into philosophy? Eastern traditions? Quantum science?"

Christine was biting her lip, trying to hold it together. It was left to her husband to confirm, "He had a deep and abiding interest in those subjects."

"He must have been an extraordinary young man." Barbara reached out to squeeze Christine's hand.

"He was," she managed, somewhat tearfully. "With such a good heart."

"So much better than mine," nodded Kroaker.

There was a lengthy pause before he looked up, meeting Steve Hartley's gaze. "You remember that deal I did with Tarsich?"

"It's transformed the industry. Especially Manolos."

"I could have taken out the brickworks myself."

"We all wondered why you didn't."

Kroaker tapped his chest. "Will's heart."

"You took the high road?"

"I was looking at your company website," Kroaker began to well up himself, and had to fight for his composure. "The thought of destroying all your livelihoods made me feel physically sick."

"I remember you coming home with that news." Christine turned to her husband. "How the company was suddenly out of the woods with Tarsich. After all the stress it was like this huge burden being lifted. You said you felt as if it was a gift from Will. D'you remember saying?"

Steve Hartley was nodding. "As if Will was looking down on us."

"Well—" Kroaker smiled "—in a way he was. Only it was more an inside job."

Both Harleys were staring at him, trying to take it all in.

From next door, in the community hall, there was some kind of commotion. Raised voices and drumming filtered into the café along with the usual traffic noises.

"I know I wouldn't have been the first person on your list to receive your son's heart," he told them, "but I can't begin to tell you how very grateful I am. Will not only gave me the chance to keep on living, he also changed who I am. I just have one question."

All three of them were studying him closely as the chorus of voices from the next-door hall became suddenly louder as a marimba band joined in.

At the counter, the Wild Ginger staff were laughing, a few breaking into African dance. Some of the customers were getting up to go next door, and on the pavement outside a stream of people were jiving their way towards the entrance.

For a moment, Christine Hartley glanced around. As she did, an African man caught sight of her. With a dazzling smile of recognition he came dancing into the café, followed by a group of others.

"*Tatenda*! *Tatenda*!" he was greeting them effusively.

"That's the name of the charity," Steve explained to the Kroakers while the man hugged Christine.

"*Tatenda* means "Thank you!" in Shona," announced the man with a smile.

In that instant, everything became clear to Ken Kroaker—the enigma of the repeating syllables. What they meant and why they had been so important to Will. Just as, he had a feeling, they were about to become important to him.

"You are coming?" The man was jiving, grabbing Christine's arm playfully as he danced. "Then we all eat."

"Why not?" Ken stood up.

The others looked at him, surprised and delighted, before they got up too. The four of them were soon dancing into the community hall, bursting with the tribal rhythms of Africa and aglow in the afternoon sun.

"*Tatenda!*" was evidently the chorus of the music being played too, because from time to time the whole crowd would sing out the word with much ululating and stamping of feet. Their exuberance was so infectious that is was impossible not to join in.

With his heart parents on one side and wife on the other, Ken Kroaker had never felt so carefree or so gloriously happy. It wasn't just the euphoria of the moment. It was also the knowledge that he had received not only a new heart, but along with it, a new understanding. A new gratitude for the preciousness of his life. A wish to move towards the love and the light.

"*Tatenda!*" he joined the group in the community hall as they danced and sang passionately. "*Tatenda!*"

"When memory is seen purely and exclusively as taking place only in the neurons of the brain, cellular memories reported by heart transplant recipients seem absurd. When it is acknowledged that all cells have a form of shared info-energetic memory and that the heart also thinks, feels, and remembers, the recall of memories from heart donors and systemic cellular memories become possible."

—PAUL PEARSALL, *PhD,*
The Heart's Code, The New Findings About Cellular Memories
and Their Role in the Mind/Body/Spirit Connection.

JUST SO

THERE WAS ONCE A NOVICE MONK WHO, EXPECTING A VISIT FROM A GREATLY revered master, spent the whole morning raking leaves off the monastery lawn. Autumn leaves had fallen in great profusion from a nearby cherry tree. When the master arrived, he took in the immaculately raked lawn, before walking over to the tree and shaking its trunk so hard that many more leaves fluttered down. Regarding the leaf-strewn lawn, he turned to the novice monk and said, "How beautiful!"
—From "Zen Tales" Editor: Venerable Goetcha Thinh Khing

Penny Perkin liked things to be "just so".

Even as a young girl she had been very particular about, for example, the way that patterned dresses should be hung on a different part of her wardrobe rail from non-patterned ones. And how the non-patterned ones were to follow the sequence of the rainbow, with lighter shades on the left graduating to darker tones on the right in the case of each individual color. She'd adopted the same, fastidious approach to her crayons, toys and other belongings, much to the surprise, and occasional exasperation, of her parents who were neither pedantic, nor casual in their way of life.

Penny was similarly conscientious at school. Whether in the classroom or on the playing field, such was her commitment to exacting standards that she would do whatever it took, practice for however long was needed, and exert herself to whatever extent was required to make sure that she achieved high grades and outstanding scores.

Fortunately for Penny, she didn't hold anyone else to the same rigorous code she demanded of herself. She even regarded her own behavior with a lightness, as though it was some bizarre quirk that made her so obsessive—a perplexing foible that she certainly wouldn't wish upon anyone else. For that reason, instead of being the kind of girl who might otherwise stir up envy and resentment among her peers, she was a popular kid who grew into a well-regarded young woman.

As a child, Penny was a voracious reader. She had a shelf stacked with many books, which she would read and re-read—with one exception. *Zen Tales* contained a story about a poor, novice monk and visiting teacher, which she found utterly repellent. Instead of appreciating the novice's efforts, the teacher seemed to throw them back in his face. Quite what the moral of *that* story was supposed to be, she couldn't possibly guess. But having read the story once, she couldn't bear to pick the book up again.

Penny found her way into accountancy, then actuarial science, her diligence and proficiency in negotiating her way among the most complex systems enabling her to float effortlessly through her studies at university, before going on to become an early achiever in the world of work.

But Penny's need for order was not always a great fit for life outside of work. Socially she enjoyed wide horizons, but romantic relationships in early adulthood came with an ambiguity and uncertainty with which she was ill at ease. Her own specific requirements, when matters turned intimate, also presented something of a challenge.

Penny couldn't abide the idea of waking up to a stranger in her bed. Or even someone who wasn't that strange, but who was, well, *there*. The sheer disruption to her mental equilibrium was enough reason to rule it out. Even worse, given her stringency in matters of personal hygiene, was having the cleanliness of her carefully ironed bed linen sullied for the sake of an intimate encounter which may— or may very well not—prove gratifying. She most certainly didn't wish to discover, first thing in the morning, stray garments or the stains of unmentionable body fluids in her pristine cotton sheets.

So when things turned hot and heavy, it was to the kitchen that she would lead her beau. There she was perfectly willing to strip naked and lie on the sterile surface of the kitchen table to receive her lover. Or alternatively, to bend over the same so that he could take her from behind. Just so long as he didn't have any unsavory ideas involving bed linen or soft furnishings.

After relations were concluded and she'd dispatched her partner home, it was only five minutes with the rubber gloves and spray-on bleach, and order would be restored to Planet Perkin.

Penny had always been as punctilious in her concern about ethics, as she was in other matters. Guided by a strong sense of probity, she always wished to do the right thing and to make sure that, in her relations with others, a sense of fairness prevailed. As a result, her life became very difficult indeed.

In her early twenties Penny watched a twenty-minute video about intensive animal farming. That brief exposure—to baby chicks being flung into a furnace by the hundred each minute because they were born male, to sows imprisoned in stalls so narrow they couldn't turn to nurse their offspring, to cattle facing terrified, mechanized death in abattoirs—had been enough to turn her vegan.

Adapting to an austere diet of which some other people were strangely resentful, even mocking, was one thing. But Penny found that not even her new, austere regime was enough to bring an end to her own contribution to animal suffering. A visit to a wildlife conservation center made her acutely aware just how massively humans had encroached on the countryside, blocking animal migration paths that had existed since time immemorial, clearing land and destroying the homes and food sources of countless beings. The demand for crops was driving the relentless expansion of the human species at the expense of thousands of others. Being a vegan, she came to learn, didn't absolve her of blame.

Like many other people, Penny was concerned about the environment. Like very few, she went to unusual lengths to minimize her own carbon footprint. She would use public transport even when it was inconvenient. In her late twenties, when she bought her first car, she paid over the odds for an electric hybrid. So she was dismayed when she discovered that the two dogs she had warm-heartedly rescued from death row at the local pound were responsible for more carbon emissions per year than if she'd owned a gas-guzzling SUV.

The same ethical conundrums seemed to apply everywhere. Shunning the evils of sugar, with its attendant specters of obesity and diabetes, she routinely drank "light" sodas—only to uncover a study showing that artificial sweeteners were associated with an increased risk of dementia. Donating to a food aid charity operating in Africa, she came to learn that food hampers were distributed only to supporters of the ruling party—was she helping prop up one of the most venal regimes on earth?

And so it went on. The same lack of moral certitude, of unambiguous rightness plagued so many choices that even deciding which was the lesser of two evils could be a bewildering and exasperating challenge. As someone who thought about her choices constantly, cared very deeply, and did her utmost to act in the interests of the greater good, Penny found it increasingly stressful trying to negotiate her way through life. To arrange things so that they were just so.

In her late 20s, with work pressures ratcheting up, Penny consulted a psychologist to deal with stress. Among his suggestions was that she take up the practice of meditation, which was how she came to attend a six-week program given at the Tibetan Buddhist Center. Penny had no particular interest in Buddhism, but as the center was only ten minutes walk from her home, and no carbon emissions would be required getting there, it was convenient.

Geshe Ling, the elderly Tibetan monk who had founded the center, had a serene presence on the teaching throne at the front of the room and seemed a tangible embodiment of what he taught. From the moment she stepped into the room, Penny had a powerful sensation that she had found a way to the order and rightness she had been seeking her whole life.

But at the same time, from that very first session he offered an approach that filled her with disquiet.

"Peace and equanimity cannot be found by trying to re-arrange the world outside us," he said, rebutting precisely what Penny had been attempting to do her whole life. "It must come from within. If we wish to develop inner peace—" he touched his heart "—we have to cultivate it here."

What about all the helpless lambs being butchered, right at this minute? Penny wanted to ask, but was too respectful to interject. What about all the people being starved to death just because they had voted the wrong way? How could she sit here, in the midst of such a world, trying to cultivate inner peace? Was it morally right even to try?

Images of meditating Buddhist monks in South East Asia crowded unbidden into her mind. They'd beg for a meal from local people, before spending much of the day meditating in the forest or the temple. Sure, they may be calm and serene, but what use were they to anyone else? Wasn't there something supremely selfish—even narcissistic—about their way of life?

"You may think that just meditating is a waste of time. A self-indulgence," he chuckled. "This is what people sometimes say. ""I have more important things to do than just sit around thinking about nothing"."

Others in the class seemed to share his amusement.

Not Penny.

"So tell me this: since when has incessant thinking solved your problems? Or anyone else's?"

Penny felt as if he was addressing her personally.

"All the worry and anxiety. The constant mental agitation. Could it be that, with a calmer mind, you could be of greater benefit to yourself and to others? If your mind was less like a snow globe—" he shook an imaginary sphere with his hand "—could you enjoy greater clarity? Coherence?"

Committed, as she was, to fairness, Penny was willing to concede that Geshe Ling had a point.

"Science agrees with Buddhism on this," he continued. "Brain scans have been done showing that we produce more gamma waves when we meditate. Gamma waves are associated with "aha" experiences. Light bulb moments. Seeing the wood for the trees. This is one of the reasons so many companies these days want their staff to learn meditation. They know we become better thinkers—more innovative, focused, productive—when we have a settled mind."

The meditation technique Geshe Ling advocated to calm the mind seemed almost absurdly simple. All you had to do was sit in a quiet room for fifteen minutes, ideally cross-legged on a cushion, focusing on the sensation of the breath at the tip of the nostrils, and counting your exhalations from one to ten. If a thought should enter your mind, you were to let go of it. Ignore it. Not allow it to disturb the focus on your breath.

Keep this up every day for six weeks, said the lama, and you would start to notice positive changes in your life. Likening mind training to physical training, he explained that, for results, one's efforts must be consistent and regular—words that appealed strongly to Penny's ingrained commitment to self-discipline.

The first time she tried meditating, during that class, Penny found little difficulty concentrating on her breath. Sure she had a few, extraneous thoughts, but she shrugged them off without too much trouble.

In the days that followed, however, she faced mental mayhem every time she sat on the appointed cushion of her sitting room. Not only were her sessions filled with distraction. She was hardly ever able to reach ten breaths without losing her count. Geshe Ling's method may be simple but, she was beginning to recognize, that didn't mean it was at all easy.

Penny wasn't alone in making this discovery. Every subsequent class in the six-week program was attended by a smaller and smaller group. And those who remained were as one in the challenge they faced.

"I want to meditate," a young woman spoke for all of them when prompted for feedback after the first week. "But my mind's just too busy. And it seems to be getting worse since I started meditating!"

Geshe Ling's presence at the front was genial and reassuring. Everyone experienced the same thing to begin with, he told them— none of them possessed uniquely busy minds. Nor had their ability to focus deteriorated. Rather, it was only now they were paying full attention to what was going on that they were recognizing the full extent of their own agitation.

"The reason that most people give up meditating is because they think their minds are too busy," he said, the pathos of this mistaken view reflected in his face for a moment. "But what if someone said to you that their body is too weak to benefit from going to the gym. That there is no point even trying because they will never get stronger. Would you agree with them? Or would you say they need more determination!" He struck his fist on the low table in front of him. "More courage! Meditation is not for sissies."

Leaning forward, that presence of oceanic tranquility revealed itself to be founded on a surprising power. "Don't become a victim of your own, weak mind. Where has self-doubt, feebleness, ever got you? No matter how many times you get distracted, keep bringing your mind back to the object. Ten days, ten months, ten years—no problem how long it takes. Think: I will not give in!"

As the six-week program progressed, Geshe Ling taught the students different methods to quieten their minds. In particular, when thoughts arose in the mind, instead of engaging with the thought, in the usual way, the students were to regard the thought as an object. Something to acknowledge, accept and let go of. "Don't be your thoughts and feelings," the lama told them. "Be the *awareness* of your thoughts and feelings. In letting go of them, imagine you're releasing the string of a helium balloon which instantly disappears into space."

"In the gap after that thought has dissolved, and before the next thought arises," said Geshe Ling. "*That* is where you find mind."

Penny persisted in her daily attempts. But she had never been able to shake off the doubts she'd had about this whole exercise, right from the beginning. Doubts she hadn't understood, let alone been able to articulate, until she'd been experimenting with it for quite some time. But once she'd worked out what they were, her concerns became more and more obvious. Troubling. And they needed to be discussed.

She booked a private session with Geshe Ling.

"I like the idea of having a calmer mind," she began. "I can see why that would be more useful."

Sitting opposite her, in his small room, late one afternoon, Geshe Ling acknowledged this with a smile, as he waited for the "but".

"But the idea of letting go of thoughts, I mean, *completely* … that can't be right, surely?"

The lama wore a gentle expression. "That's what we're attempting."

"What happens if you have a really important thought? A useful thought? Surely you shouldn't let go when that happens?"

"All thought." He nodded. "We let go of. To say a thought is "useful" or "important" is making a judgment about it. And to make a judgment, we have to think. When we meditate, we are practicing non-thinking."

It was precisely such circular arguments and an unwillingness to accept any thought as important that troubled Penny. "It just seems to me," she said, somewhat tetchily, "that you would rather we didn't think at all!"

Meeting her eyes, Geshe Ling burst out laughing. "There's not much chance of that happening, is there?" he chuckled. Then seeing that Penny didn't share his amusement, he went on. "In general our problem is too much thinking," he said. "When we meditate, we practice letting go of thought. This equips us for when we're not meditating, to free ourselves of unwanted cognition."

He was confirming her darkest concerns.

"But what happens if I feel my thoughts are right?" she asked. "*And* important?"

"Do they disturb your peace of mind?" he asked.

"Sometimes," she replied, nodding, thinking about an article she had only just read about religious persecution in Sudan. "Very often."

"Then best to let go of them," said the lama.

"But to let go of them I'd be letting go of my concern for others. Of my wish for fairness and decency. This is who I am. Are you asking me to give up my whole sense of identity?"

There it was! Penny had finally managed to spell out what was troubling her about meditation. "To be honest, I have doubts about this whole process. Big doubts."

Geshe Ling allowed silence to amplify what she had just said, as he regarded her with a gentle smile. The stillness of the twilight filling the room seemed to lend clarity to what she had just said, and to reveal the anguish from which it had arisen—a conflict she described with impressive precision.

When the lama responded, it was not as she had expected. "This is excellent!" he told her. "You are making good progress! Small doubts lead to small breakthroughs. Big doubts to big breakthroughs."

Breakthroughs, large or small, weren't what Penny had in mind, at that moment. Putting her concerns into words seemed to give them a certainty that deepened her conviction she had been right all along. Never had she felt more at odds with the man seated opposite.

"This sense of identity," he said softly. "It is not your physical body you're talking of?"

"No, no." She shook her head, wondering why he was being obtuse.

"So it's a concept?"

She shrugged. "I s'pose." She had never given much thought to what a person's identity consisted of exactly.

"Do other people have the same concept of you that you do?"

Penny knew for a fact that they didn't. Only that day she'd been called "anal" for throwing out ice from a glass in a café she'd never visited before. She had read horror stories about ice contamination and just didn't see that it was worth the risk. Her "prudent" was other people's "persnickety'. "Other people don't see things, don't see me, the way I do," she told the lama.

"So this concept of yourself which you don't want to lose. It's one that only you have?"

Again, she felt in deep waters. "I suppose."

"It's a concept that causes you to suffer?"

"Yes," she nodded, suddenly starting to feel quite tearful.

"So why cling to it?"

In her mind she found herself fast-forwarding from the dresses, carefully arranged in her childhood wardrobe, to her time at university. Her career as a disciplined, compassionate, stressed-out executive striving for fairness for everyone—and never getting close. "If I give all that up, I have nothing!" she welled up. "Is that just ego? Am I resisting the death of my own ego?"

Reaching over, Geshe Ling took her hand between his own soft, warm palms and held it. "When a child grows into an adult, does the child die?"

She shook her head.

"The child matures. We all need to mature in our understanding of who we really are. It is not this bundle of ideas and conditioning we hold so tightly. Tell me, my dear, when you meditate, have you ever caught a glimpse of the gaps between thoughts? Between concepts?"

Wiping her eyes with her other hand, Penny nodded. "Here," she acknowledged. "When we meditate here, in class, with you."

The quality of the meditation she experienced in Geshe Ling's presence was, she knew, of a different order compared to when she tried on her own at home.

"And how does that feel?" He squeezed her hand, before letting go of it.

"Peaceful," she said. "Clear."

"Without boundaries?"

"Yes."

"The sense of self we cling to, the stories we tell ourselves about ourselves, this is a false "I". And our main problem, as humans, is that we are all "I" specialists."

Despite herself, Penny couldn't help smiling.

"Each one of us is an expert on this "I". Where it was born and brought up. The triumphs or failings of "I". What "I" believe about this or that. But when we search for this "I" we cannot find it. Because it is only a concept. An idea we have about ourselves, which is different from everyone else's idea about ourselves. An idea which can suddenly and completely change.

"If we wish to find freedom, we must first let go of this false "I". Of all concepts about it. After letting go, we discover that mind still exists. That consciousness is infinite and lucid and tranquil. And if we can abide there for long enough, through training, that tranquility deepens into a state of abiding bliss. This bag of bones with all its self-important ideas, this is not, ultimately, who "I" am at all."

Absorbed in the lama's words, which he communicated to her at a heart level as well as out loud, Penny encountered a more panoramic version of herself than she had ever guessed at. One which went beyond anything she had ever imagined.

"Changing this idea of who and what I am," she spoke somewhat hesitantly. "How does that help those who suffer?"

"You have a very good heart, Penny. I could see that the first time you came here." It was the first time that Geshe Ling had used her name, and the fact that he had done so in recognizing her compassion made her glow.

"Our ability to help others depends on our power, does it not?"

She nodded.

"Our capacity as human beings is very limited. Yes, we may be able to help some beings here, to rescue others there. And we should try. But we cannot really offer a permanent solution. On the other hand as fully enlightened beings, there are no limits to the help we can provide. This is exactly why we strive to become enlightened—not only for our own sakes, but to help all others too.

"If you motivate your practice with, for example, a wish to free all animals from imprisonment in narrow cells. Permanently. To uplift poor people without rewarding dictators. To stop people being persecuted because of their beliefs ..." as he checked through the list of some of her most anguished or recent concerns she realized the man sitting opposite her had an extraordinary insight into her mind "... use all your loving kindness like rocket fuel to propel you in your journey towards enlightenment. This is the meaning of bodhichitta, the ultimate purpose of loving kindness: the wish to achieve enlightenment in order to help all others attain the same state."

Penny left her session with Geshe Ling inspired. In a profound way, something inside her had shifted. It would take time to process the implications of letting go of the myth of self. The self that seemed so all important but, when it came down to it, was only an idea, or a collection of ideas, none of them permanent.

And she finished the six-week introductory course, feeling more calm, coherent and settled than she had for a long time.

But then she went away on a week-long vacation. And when she returned, things at work went crazy, and her mother fell ill, and without a daily routine she no longer meditated.

Before she knew it, she had reverted to her usual, stressed-out self. One who had tasted the benefits of a tranquil mind and, deep down, had a yearning to re-experience it. But one for whom the practice, like a secret river, had disappeared underground.

When she thought back, even to that meeting with Geshe Ling, although she remembered it as profoundly life-enhancing, when she tried to remember the concepts that had given her such release, or recapture the incredible lightness that she had felt at the time, she was unable to. Whatever it was she had grasped when she had been with him, now somehow eluded her. Like a slippery fish that she had once held in her hands, it was now just a flash of light in her memory.

Months passed.

Penny slid into her well-worn ways of being, striving relentlessly for order in all things. Feeling combustible emotions of anguish and outrage whenever she encountered injustice. And experiencing tense times with her boyfriend, Neil, for whom the erotic possibilities of the kitchen table—the spatulas notwithstanding—were beginning to wane.

Then one day, attending a work convention in a different city, Penny found herself eating lunch with a colleague from another office. Conversation turned to stress management and the colleague told her that her life had been changed by meditation. Specifically, repeating a particular Buddhist mantra.

After Penny returned home, her colleague sent her a short book about the practice, which Penny read over the weekend. The book reminded her how she'd benefited from meditating and encouraged her to take it up again.

Mantra recitation had been one of several different types of meditation that Geshe Ling had shared with the class, and it had resonated with her. The particular mantra recommended in the book, was lengthy, multi-syllabic and written in Sanskrit—learning it off by heart was exactly the kind of intellectual challenge that Penny found bracing. She duly set about becoming completely familiar with it.

The book also emphasized the importance of receiving teachings about the mantra from a qualified lama. Geshe Ling was exactly such a lama, but Penny felt embarrassed, having not shown her face at the center for quite some time.

She was sitting, reading a section of the mantra book in her local coffee shop one evening when she became aware of a presence beside her table. Looking up, who should she find standing right there, but Geshe Ling.

"Good evening." She rose to her feet. She was unsure of how to act, but the lama quickly waved at her to sit. As she was so doing, it occurred to her to say that this was an astonishing coincidence, before quickly registering that it was nothing of the kind.

"You like this book?" He nodded towards the cover.

"I am really enjoying it." She smiled. "I'd like to learn." She glanced down at the cover, self-conscious. "I need a teacher and I wonder if you would consider ..."

"Of course!" said Geshe Ling. "I know just the teacher for you."

"Oh." This wasn't quite what Penny had expected.

"It would mean you'd have to travel."

Making an effort to reach an appropriate teacher was, Penny had read in the book, highly auspicious. Unlike contemporary views of convenience, the idea was that the more arduous and challenging the journey to visit a teacher, the greater the benefit.

She nodded. "Okay."

Geshe Ling looked at her with the sweetest of smiles. "Good," he said. "I suggest you consult with Tashi Tsering. He is widely recognized as one of the foremost practitioners of this method in the world today. Not only that—" Geshe Ling leaned towards her, confidentially "—he is a one of the most remarkable meditation yogis of our age. It is said that he can effortlessly manifest the siddhis, or special powers, that accompany supreme attainment. I can make the necessary arrangements for you to see him."

"Thank you!" Penny nodded. "Where does he live?"

"On a small island called Ladalisha."

"Ladalisha?"

"In India."

Penny blanched.

India was everything that caused Penny to feel troubled. It was chaotic on a scale that defied description. Heartbreaking inequality was on display at every street corner where beggars in rags reached their bony arms to the tinted windows of passing luxury cars. Pain and suffering could be neither denied nor resolved.

Almost overwhelmed by the sensory overload, Penny made her way to Ladalisha guided by an escort Geshe Ling had arranged—a cousin of his, it turned out, called Dawa, who worked in the travel business. Her long-haul flight followed by a grueling, six-hour train journey, by the end of that first day, Penny was so exhausted that she fell fast asleep on her hotel bed, even though she hadn't shrouded it in the anti-bacterial, hypo allergenic mattress protector she had brought especially for this purpose.

Next day, she was guided by Dawa to the island. Ladalisha was not, at all, what she had expected. Instead of the beautifully landscaped haven in which she imagined a holy man at one with the verdant landscape and fluting calls of forest birds, it was a garbage-strewn thicket on the other side of a swamp. There was only one way to get across—to row. And because Geshe Ling's cousin had other business to attend to that day, Penny was left to row herself.

"Don't be worried, ma'am," Dawa assured her, showing her into a small rowing boat of much the same kind people hired on ornamental lakes in city parks around the world. "You will easily find Tashi Tsering. It is only a small island." He smiled broadly. "And he is the one with a face like a monkey."

Drawing on all her emotional reserves, Penny battled with the creaking boat, did her best to ignore the stench of the polluted water, and, slowly and shakily, made her way to a mooring on the other side.

Because the island was no bigger than a football pitch, and Tashi Tsering was the only person living on it, Penny's task to find him was not a difficult one.

But it was confronting.

Spotting the weather-beaten figure sitting on his haunches before a small fire in a clearing, she noticed how he wore rags for clothes. How his unshaven face that was, indeed, like that of a monkey. He appeared deep in thought as she approached, the crackle of leaves and branches as she stepped closer seeming not to distract him.

Being super-polite, Penny was uncertain what to do next. She was close enough to see that his lips were moving. She could even hear him chanting. She caught snatches of the mantra about which she had come to consult him—but she didn't want to interrupt him in mid flow—a mala rosary dangled from his hand. Perhaps he was counting his mantras?

Without looking up directly, Tashi Tsering gestured with his arm for her to come closer. Penny did so, squatting on the other side of the burning embers, regarding him closely as he continued his recitation.

Being familiar with the mantra, as she paid attention, tuning in exactly to what he was saying, she suddenly went cold. It was a heavy feeling, one of such profound disappointment that she felt herself sinking towards the ground.

She didn't want to believe her own ears. She strained to listen, wanting to catch herself out, prove herself wrong. But there could be no denying it. She hadn't misheard him. As he repeated the mantra, time and again, she had to deal with the stark reality: Tashi Tsering was saying it wrong!

Not for the first time she wondered what craziness had persuaded her to make this trip in the first place. India with all its problems. Precious time away from work. Coming here had gone against all her conditioning but she had allowed herself to hope, to believe that something transformational may occur, that she'd have some magical, mystical experience that would change her whole life.

What a fool she had been! What a gullible little idiot! All that she had ended up with, in the middle of this squalid little lake, was a rag-clad derelict who hadn't even learned his lines!

Penny raised herself to her feet and about-turned. Not taking too much care about the noise she made, she pushed her way through brittle branches, away from the so-called expert, and back towards her boat. She was almost there when she heard him call out, "Hello!"

It was a brief exchange. Tashi Tsering got up from where he had been sitting and came towards her. Having disturbed his session, she supposed she owed him an explanation for her visit.

"Geshe Ling suggested I come to see you," she said. "I was going to ask you for teachings about the mantra. But you are saying it wrong."

His eyes widened for a moment. "Wrong?" he repeated.

"At the end. You are missing out "*Hum ah peh*"."

"You think?"

Not masking her impatience, Penny undid the clasp of the handbag strapped around her neck, brought out the book she had been reading, and turned to the relevant page, in which the mantra appeared in bold print. She read it out, in a loud voice, for Tashi Tsering's benefit, enunciating every Sanskrit syllable precisely as her finger ran underneath each word.

He nodded.

She shrugged. "Doesn't seem much point in me staying," she observed, her tone one of bitter disappointment.

Climbing back in the boat, Tashi Tsering silently helped her untether it, and gave her a helpful push away from the island. She began to row, her attempts laborious and ineffectual.

She had been rowing for some time, not getting very far, when she suddenly heard Tashi Tsering's voice. "You are saying the way to pronounce the mantra is like this?" he asked, before reciting it the way she had suggested.

She turned to find him seeming to walk on the water beside her. He was standing there, in broad daylight, defying gravity, reason, and her whole sense of what was possible.

Taking in what was happening, looking him up and down in total disbelief, when she glanced at his face, he was smiling. As their eyes met, he started to laugh.

She couldn't help herself. Sharing the humor of the crazy, amazing, unbelievable situation, she had to laugh too.

And when their chuckles subsided, and he climbed in the boat and sat opposite, Tashi Tsering told her:

"The power of a mantra doesn't come from the words used," he chuckled. "It's from the faith with which they are recited."

Penny returned to the island and spent the rest of that day in the presence of her monkey-faced tutor. After a while in his presence she ceased to see his features as simian, or the island as squalid or the swamp as toxic. Instead, from those very first words about the power of the mantra, she was drawn in by his teachings, which he communicated with an authenticity that came from the heart. And along with the specific instructions he gave her, beneath the ebb and flow of his words, at a deeper level he reminded her of all that Geshe Ling had revealed to her when they had met: most of all, the importance of letting go. Letting go of her deeply ingrained ideas about the need for things to be just so, whether that was the way a mantra should be said, or the arrangement of the dresses in her wardrobe. Letting go of her passionately held views about the way that things should be in a chaotic, unjust and constantly changing world. Letting go, most of all, of that powerful sense of self—one that, impossible to find on analysis, returned at messianic full throttle, the moment she turned her back on it.

If she really wished to help others, she was reminded that she first had to deal with her own demons. She may, for a long time, have believed that if she could get everything the way she so earnestly believed it should be, then life would be fine and dandy. But she realized now that there was no way to control the uncontrollable in her own life, let alone in the lives of others. True peace comes not from trying to get things the way you want them, but from connecting to the way they are. Only when compassion is based on this connection, can it have any real power.

Penny retained these same recognitions when she returned home. Motivated by Tashi Tsering, meditation became a daily priority, the foundation of all that she did in the world.

She was soon a regular at the Buddhist center. Much less of a stress-head at work. And no longer so wracked with indignation or distress every time she encountered some fresh injustice.

One Thursday evening she was on the phone to her boyfriend, Neil. "What about coming over tomorrow night and I'll cook some pasta," she offered. Friday evenings at her place had been a frequent fixture in the past. This time, however, she was proposing something different, "If you like, you can stay over."

At the other end, Neil was hesitant. "How do you mean?"

"Spend the night."

"Yes," his confusion deepened. "But, I mean, where?"

"In my bed."

There was the longest pause from the other end as her boyfriend tried to get his head around this radical suggestion. Looking for a catch. Before he asked, "Are you saying what I think you're saying?"

"You'll have to come over to see." She laughed. "Don't forget your toothbrush."

That Sunday, Penny's father dropped off a trunk at her house. Her parents were downsizing, and as part of their clear-out, they wanted to let her have some of her childhood memorabilia—items they'd had in storage just in case, one day, she had children of her own she wanted to share them with. Despite Penny's insistence that they dump the trunk on the verge for the next municipal bulk garbage collection, they wanted her to make that call.

On Sunday afternoon she did her household laundry—including sheets which had, indeed, been stained with unmentionable body fluids, both on Friday and Saturday nights. As the sheets churned and tumbled in the washing machine, Penny made herself a cup of single origin, fair-trade, organic coffee, opened the trunk and went through items she hadn't seen in over 20 years.

She smiled, fondly, as she held the faded, soft toys of her childhood. She remembered afternoons in her cubby-house playing some of the puzzles. And as her finger ran down the spines of the books she had read, tightly packed along the bottom of the trunk, she paused as she reached one particular volume, before drawing it out.

In a flash she was back on the day that she had first opened it up, and was reading the story of the novice monk. Even now, her heart quickened at the memory of the way that the greatly revered master had gone directly over to the cherry tree and shaken it till leaves scattered across the pristine lawn.

Only, this time as she read it, she laughed. Throwing back her head, she snorted as she did only in moments of spontaneous and deeply felt humor.

It may have taken her all of her life to understand, she thought, but she got it! The revered master hadn't been the inscrutable sadist she had been imagining, all these years, but a teacher who had been revealing a simple truth: that the lawn had already been beautiful. Even in the midst of chaos and disharmony, even when things are most definitely not "just so', it is still a wonderful world!

THE ISLAND OF JEWELS

Like a trader gone to an island of Jewels
Returning home empty-handed,
Without the paths of the ten virtues
You will not obtain it again in future.
—*Aryasura, 2nd-century Buddhist poet*

ONCE UPON A TIME THERE WAS A POOR MAN CALLED DEPA WHO found himself transported to the island of jewels. Depa had no idea what to expect of this fabled place, but as he arrived he saw that the long, white beaches skirting the island were strewn with jewels. Rubies, diamonds, emeralds and sapphires, some the size of grapefruits, glittered like a dazzling necklace as far as the eye could see. Washed up by the ocean onto the pristine sands, they were freely available to anyone who wanted to pick them up. Interspersed with stones, shells and other ocean detritus, not all of the jewels were of the same quality. But Depa knew that even one of them would be sufficient to transform his life.

As for cramming the satchel he was carrying with the finest quality jewels, well—that would bring riches beyond his wildest imaginings. Staring at the jewel-strewn beaches, Depa could hardly believe his eyes.

Like all visitors, Depa was required to attend island school for twenty minutes to be taught about the rules and customs governing the island. He soon discovered that the rules were very simple. There were only three:

1. All visitors to the island of jewels arrived and departed alone.

2. Visitors could not take anything from the island when they left—except for their *collection* of precious jewels.

3. Visits to the island could not exceed 24 hours duration, but visitors may be required to leave at any time, without notice.

As for island customs, these were many and elaborate and mainly concerned the buying and selling of goods and services. All such transactions were to be carried out in the local currency, which must be earned. As Depa left the orientation session and went out into the island streets, he discovered all manner of commercial activities briskly underway—and no shortage of bars, restaurants and other places where day trippers were enjoying themselves.

A very small group of visitors made their way straight down to the beach, where they began carefully examining the precious jewels that had washed up overnight, selecting only the largest, unflawed examples to put in their rucksacks. But most day trippers, having taken in the flurry of important busyness in the streets and the many attractions on offer, began to focus their energies on earning the money they needed for meals and entertainment.

Depa had noticed a curious thing beginning to happen during his time at school. His memory of life before the island began to fade. So much so that he was soon struggling to remember even the most basic facts, like the twenty years he had spent working as a blacksmith. It wasn't long before the idea of any kind of existence beyond this place took on the quality of a dream. His wife and children, his mother, siblings and extended family were quickly forgotten. It was as if his consciousness had only really begun once he'd arrived on the island.

"I'm Bill the Bike Tour Man!" A jovial fellow at a bicycle hire stall called out to him. "Come and work for me! Two hours of servicing bikes will earn you enough for all your needs!"

"Thank you!" replied Depa, having to step aside to avoid a woman with piercing, turquoise eyes who was hurrying from school towards the beach as fast as her stubby legs would carry her. There was something vaguely familiar about her short, bustling figure, but he couldn't place exactly what. As he watched her reach the sand and begin combing through the seaweed and worthless stones to pick out an exquisite ruby, Depa wondered if he, himself, should be doing exactly the same thing. But when he glanced back at Bill, and saw the expression on the bike tour operator's face, he paused. Bill was shaking his head in droll amusement.

"Newcomers!" He smiled at Depa in a knowing manner that seemed to confer a privileged, insider status on him. "It's pitiful the way some of them get so carried away."

Bill's emphatic manner took Depa by surprise. "Perhaps they are just trying to make the most of their short time here?" he suggested.

The other's eyes narrowed. "They'll soon learn the hard way that their precious jewels are not legal tender in this part of the world. If you want to eat you have to work. No work and you go hungry, or become a burden to others. It really is that simple."

Depa couldn't fault Bill's logic. Jewels or no jewels, he *would* have to eat in the next 24 hours. Nonetheless, he couldn't avoid the knowledge that if he was to accept Bill's job he would be setting his priorities. Making a choice. One he very much hoped he wasn't going to regret.

After checking wages and confirming that Bill was offering a fair rate, Depa agreed to work for him for the next two hours.

It was enjoyable employment given Depa's affinity for mechanics. And the bonus was that he got to hear about the island from people who were returning their bicycles having toured all around it. He learned where the most prized sapphires were to be found, as well as the place where massive, flawless diamonds littered the beach in great profusion. All visitors spoke about the awe-inspiring beauty of Trance Cove, where forested mountains descended to a broad, sweep of beach, and, nestling into the lush, forest canopy were restaurants, gardens and luxurious, private gazebos, where people could take in the spectacular vistas while indulging in whatever sense pleasures they wished. Trance Cove was expensive, however, and Depa quickly calculated that if he wanted to enjoy its manifold delights he'd have to work not for two, but for four hours.

He was contemplating exactly this when he heard a commotion outside the shop, and he looked up to see a man being escorted down the street, flanked by two ethereal figures in white.

"It's not fair!" The man was distraught. "I haven't even been here an hour!"

His escorts, impassive and unresponsive, continued smoothly on their way, appearing to glide just above the ground as they whisked him off, who knew where.

As they did, a woman at the side of the street with wild, raven locks and a sparkling nose-stud, and who was wearing a backpack so crammed with jewels that the straps tethering it were straining on the last hole, murmured out loud, "If only he could have spent even just one minute on the beach!"

Depa looked over at her expression of pathos.

"Do you think that time spent on the beach gives more happiness than time spent at Trance Cove?" he asked.

She turned to him with a smile. "They are two, different happinesses," she said. "The happiness at Trance Cove comes from what you get. The happiness at the beach comes from what you give. One is superficial and passes quickly. The other transforms your mind and endures."

Depa considered this for a moment before saying, "But you haven't given away any of your jewels yet."

"True," she said, nodding. "But I have collected them with the intention that others, as well as I, myself, may benefit. And that is the best use of our short time here. The source of greatest contentment."

What the woman said got Depa thinking. Even though he had long since forgotten any kind of existence before arriving on the island, the words she spoke resonated with something deep inside him—a subconscious memory perhaps, or some heartfelt impulse.

"She has a point," he said to his co-worker, Trent, who, standing next to him, had witnessed the scene.

"Sure." Trent shrugged equivocally. "But the guy being taken away was very unlucky."

"He was?"

"Most people get to stay a whole lot longer." He spoke with confidence. "The average is twenty-two hours."

Depa took a deep breath and exhaled slowly. "That's good to know," he said. "For a moment I was beginning to worry ..."

"Oh, you don't want to pay too much attention to the ascetics."

Depa hadn't heard the term before, but wasn't about to admit his ignorance. "You don't?"

Trent shook his head. "All gloom and doom with some of them. Glass half empty. But just look at us: we're here on this beautiful island with the whole day ahead of us! There's plenty of time to go collecting jewels later, if that's what you choose. Everything in its time and a time for everything."

Depa felt greatly relieved. And all the more open to the offer he soon received from his employer, Bill.

"Depa." Bill placed a hand on his shoulder and regarded him warmly. "You have been a most diligent service man and an important part of my success."

During the time Depa had been working for him, Bill had acquired an empty property next door and turned it into a thriving food and drink stall, serving much-needed refreshments to customers returning their bikes.

"I would like to promote you to Chief Bicycle Serviceman with a pay increase of twenty percent with immediate effect."

Most diligent! 20 percent! Unused to such appreciation, Depa basked in the glow of his boss's approval. In light of the reassuring exchange with Trent, he felt that this was an opportune moment to ask, "Can I stay on for another two hours?"

"Of course!" Bill readily agreed. "We make a good team, you and me." Then smiling playfully he added, "Perhaps you have heard about the legendary delights of Trance Cove?"

"I have," admitted Depa.

Bill laughed out loud. "I'll make you a man of the island yet!"

Depa's next two hours were busy, and at the end of them he collected his wages. Bill tried to persuade him to stay for another shift, but Depa's mind was made up. Besides, he was starting to feel hungry. Having worked hard all morning he felt that he had earned a decent meal. He deserved it! In the afternoon, he decided, he could turn his attention to collecting jewels. In fact, there seemed something appropriate about that time of day for jewel collection. "Everything in its time, and a time for everything," as Trent had said, the poetic cadence of the line imbuing it with a sense of profound wisdom.

Depa discovered that Trance Cove more than lived up to its reputation. Not only was the scenery more exquisitely beautiful than words could describe. The air itself had a deeply tranquillizing quality so that no sooner had you arrived in the place than you never wanted to leave. Not only had Depa completely forgotten his life and persona, his likes and dislikes before arriving on the island, even during the course of his stay he had grown and changed, and was now completely at ease with the ways of the island. At Trance Cove he observed groups of people lingering in the gardens, the wealthier ones making their way into one of the restaurants or entertainment venues. Those who hadn't earned so much seemed to live vicariously through their peers, or perhaps hoped to be invited to a party by a wealthy friend.

In an alcove fresh with the aromas of spring freesias and Himalaya pine, Depa encountered a beautiful, gold-haired woman on whose shoulder an Amazonian parrot fluttered down from a tree, brushing her cheek gently with his head, before taking off again.

The woman laughed, and as she did, her eyes met Depa's.

"He liked you!" chuckled Depa.

"That's never happened to me before!" Her eyes were bright.

The two of them fell into easy conversation and very soon Depa knew Alice well enough to invite her to join him for lunch.

He was interested to see that in the restaurant they chose, a number of ascetics were also enjoying lavish meals, including the woman with the raven hair and glittering nose stud. Being an ascetic and enjoying the pleasures of the island were not, it seemed, incompatible activities. On the contrary, Depa couldn't avoid a twinge of envy as he observed those who looked as though they were enjoying the best of both possible worlds.

As he and Alice savored delicious food in a location of exquisite beauty, while caught up in the heady fervor of burgeoning romance—yes, things moved fast on the island of jewels—Depa spent a lot longer on the meal than he had envisaged. And when lunch was over, and Alice and he were as one in their wish to take things to the next level, he rented a private gazebo. There the two of them connected rapturously and repeatedly throughout the afternoon, their love-making interspersed by interludes of short naps and chilled champagne, and accompanied by the rolling sound of waves pounding along the bay, each fresh wave flinging ashore copious quantities of fresh jewels from the ocean deep.

Some time after 4 pm, Depa caressed the naked thigh of the beauty in his arms and said, "Feel like going to collect some precious jewels from the beach?"

Jewel collection was not a subject they had discussed so far in their urgent search for intimacy. And Depa was somewhat surprised by her answer.

"No," she replied, sleepily.

"Later, then?" he asked.

"I'm not really into that … stuff."

For a moment he stopped caressing.

"But I wouldn't want to stop you," she said. "If you think it's important."

Depa was, at once, grateful for her open-mindedness, as well as curious about her disinterest. "Don't you want to leave here with as many jewels as you can?" he asked.

Propping herself up on an elbow, Alice brushed back a fallen lock of blonde hair. "Do you believe we really go somewhere else after this?" she asked.

Depa raised his eyebrows. "I've seen people being taken away with my own eyes."

"Oh sure," she agreed. "Goes on all the time. But where do you think they are taken?"

"To wherever they came from?" shrugged Depa.

"I don't remember coming from anywhere. Do you?" She asked this less as a challenge and more out of genuine curiosity.

Depa paused, trying to penetrate the thick fog of amnesia that had settled over his mind, before shaking his head. "No, I don't," he admitted. "But perhaps the jewels will be useful wherever we go."

Alice moved her head from one side to the other as if this wasn't much of an answer. "Have you ever met someone who has come back from wherever we go?"

Again, Depa had to shake his head.

"If there is such a place, I don't think whoever runs it would be so cruel as to punish people just because they didn't spend two minutes picking up a few jewels."

"I hear what you're saying." Depa had no answer to this point either. "I guess I just have this ... feeling."

"Well, off you go then." She smiled at him, as though indulging a child. "I'll still be here when you get back."

It was 5:30 pm and the light was beginning to fade when Depa finally set out for the beach with his empty satchel. A short distance from the gazebo, he encountered an elderly ascetic with a bulging backpack lying on the ground. He wore a gentle, benevolent expression, but there was no escaping the growling sounds coming from his stomach. Depa instantly recollected the words of his former employer Bill, about becoming a burden to others. Nevertheless, taking pity on the fellow and, having more than enough money for his own needs, he reached down and handed him some cash to buy a meal. So effusive were the old man's thanks that they made Depa feel like the most generous of philanthropists.

Further on, at the side of the track, Depa came across an evangelist of a kind he hadn't encountered before.

"Don't be led astray by the emeralds on the beach!" the strident woman cried. "They may have an alluring gleam, but they are worthless when you leave here!"

Shrinking away from this forceful creature, Depa soon found himself confronted by another evangelist. "Unless you accept diamonds alone as your personal jewel of choice," proclaimed the fellow with passionate conviction, "you are doomed to burn in hell from the moment they cart you away!"

Rebounding in shock, Depa was soon faced with a man wearing a far-away look in his eyes. "We are the Sapphire Children! The Chosen Ones. Only the Sapphire Covenant can protect you on Judgment Day!"

Dazed and confused, Depa quickly retraced his steps back towards the gazebos.

It just so happened that as he did so, who should he encounter climbing out of the longest stretch limo he had ever seen, but bike shop Bill. Clutching a bottle of champagne, Bill had a very attractive woman draped over each arm and was making his unsteady way towards a very opulent-looking gazebo.

"Depa, my friend! What's the matter?" Bill greeted him warmly.

Depa was relieved to have the opportunity to unburden himself. He told Bill exactly what he had just experienced.

"The reason they disagree is because they're all charlatans," Bill told him, swaying slightly. "Frauds. Con artists. If their so-called precious jewels really had any value, they would all agree. But they don't. It's a gigantic hoax! People make up all kinds of stories because they want to believe there is life off the island. Their egos can't stand the idea that our stay here is finite. Take it from me, my friend, the island is all there is."

Glancing in the direction that Depa was heading he gave him a side-long look. "Have you met anyone special?"

"An amazing woman called Alice."

"Then go back to her!" he exhorted him. "Friends, loved ones, relationships. That's what life here is all about!" He clutched the two women on each side to him who giggled. "Oh, and a bit of this doesn't hurt," he announced, holding up the bottle of champagne.

They all laughed.

Making his way back to his gazebo, Depa encountered the elderly ascetic to whom he had made a donation. The old man was spooning a rice-based meal from a wooden bowl into his mouth with great relish.

"May I ask you a question, my friend?" asked Depa.

"I'm not very knowledgeable," said the other, "but you may ask me whatever you like."

"I want to know why you think these jewels are precious?" He gestured towards the bulging backpack.

"Aha!" The other smiled. "When I began collecting them, I thought that they were."

Something in the man's manner led Depa to think that his belief had shifted.

"So, you no longer believe that?"

"Sort of. But not exactly. You see, it's not the jewels themselves that have any inherent value. It's the act of collecting them that does. The more time you spend doing this, the more your mind is transformed, little by little. An enlightened mind is the ultimate source of wealth for yourself as well as for others."

Depa was taken aback by this explanation. It had never occurred to him that the true value of the precious jewels lay in the practice of their collection, rather than in the jewels themselves. Yet the truth of what the old man said seemed self-evident in his aura of benevolent well-being.

It was also why he felt he could ask the ascetic, "Those people who accost you on the way to the beach—" his eyes were clouded with confusion "—some of them say that *this* is the only jewel worth collecting. Others directly contradict them, saying you should only focus on *that*. Who should I believe?"

"Did you notice if any of them had actually collected any of the jewels they recommend?" asked the other with a wry smile.

Startled, Depa shook his head.

"Well, do," suggested the old man, devouring another spoon of rice.

Depa couldn't wait to do exactly this. But there was still something he needed to know. "Forgetting what all those people say, which of the jewels is *really* the most precious?"

The old man smiled and after the longest pause, looked him directly in the eye. "The one that is most precious to you," he said.

"It doesn't matter which you choose?"

"Each jewel is precious to different people for different reasons according to their background and temperament. What matters is to collect them. Concern yourself with what *you* do, not with the jewel collecting of others."

Depa returned to the beach. The sun's rays were lengthening, the fading light at the end of the day making it less easy to discern one item on the beach from another. On the pathway, Depa once again encountered an evangelical, vehement in advocating rubies as the only jewel worth having.

"Do you actually possess any rubies?" asked Depa, glancing around the man's feet for signs of a ruby-laden bag, but finding none.

"I believe in rubies!" the other countered powerfully, spittle flying from his lips. "The *Book of Ruby* says that only those who cleave to rubies will have eternal life!"

"Wouldn't it be a good idea to collect some, if that's what you believe?" asked Depa.

"Such arrogance!" The evangelist grabbed him by the shirt front. "We are mere mortals, don't you understand? Mortals who are black with sin! No matter how many rubies we collect on this island we can never be redeemed! The only thing that matters is what you *believe*! Only the grace of the love of ruby can save you!"

Depa tore himself away from the man's clutches and hurried down to the beach. As he did he passed the most impassioned advocates for all the other jewels. Just as the old man had suggested, each seemed to place far more emphasis on word rather than deed.

None of them possessed the old man's presence of boundless peace.

Depa found himself a patch of sand some distance from other collectors. He lowered himself to the sand on all fours. He was about to start searching through whatever the most recent waves had brought up from the ocean, when two ethereal figures clad in white appeared on each side of him.

Depa pleaded to be allowed just one minute to find a jewel. The beings in white didn't speak—at least, not out loud. But they gave him enough time to pick up just one, smooth object about the size of an orange, and drop it in his satchel before whisking him away. It was communicated that this reprieve was on account of his generosity towards the elderly ascetic whose meal he had paid for.

Because of the gathering darkness, however, Depa had no idea if he had just picked up a glittering diamond of extraordinary value—or a worthless piece of rock.

Depa was on his way home after another long day at the black-smith's. The moon had risen much higher in the sky than was usual even on his lengthiest shifts. Two hours had gone missing. He instinctively knew where.

Time on the island of jewels went very much more quickly than in conventional reality. A whole day on the island was the equivalent of just a couple of hours of his customary, grinding existence. Exactly how he had got to the island, or returned from it, was a mystery.

The fact was that he had.

Immediately he began undoing the straps of the small, leather satchel he carried to and from work each day. Usually it contained only whatever frugal provisions he had taken with him to eat. But as he unpicked the straps with trembling fingers, he couldn't help wondering if, this evening, it might contain something else.

It did not.

There was only the empty metal bowl and lid in which he carried his midday meal.

By the time he returned home, his mother was already in her bed, a pile of burlap on the ground of their shared room. From time to time she moaned softly in her sleep, as she had for years, as though expressing a pain inexpressible in wakefulness. His wife, Leila, looked up at him, her expression both anxious as well as weary after a day picking through the city's garbage for anything that might be eaten, used or sold.

"Working so late?" She shook her head.

"Big order." He could hardly bear to meet her eyes. And as he sat on the ground around the embers of a small fire, he couldn't bring himself to look at the dirt-smudged faces of his three children, or the careworn expressions of his other relatives who were huddling together for warmth.

He closed his eyes, not so much from fatigue, but because he was overwhelmed by the day's events. He didn't know exactly how he'd been through what had happened, or even why. He only knew that he'd been granted an opportunity of great rarity.

And he felt that he had somehow failed.

He remembered—as if he was there right now—standing in his room at Trance Cove, glancing from Alice's naked limbs, across the jewel-strewn beach outside, while raising a glass of champagne, feeling the bubbles explode against his nose.

If he'd make different choices, he reflected, things could have been different right now. But instead of following his deepest, most heartfelt instincts, he had allowed himself to be distracted. Instead of being wise, he had been too willing to follow convention. It was curious how what was true, and what really mattered to him, had been so obscured beneath a fog of forgetfulness all the while he had been on the island of jewels. But now that he had returned to reality, the foolishness of the choices he had made was inescapable.

That same recognition haunted him in the weeks and months of wearying toil that followed. He had a great many questions about his visit to the island of jewels, of course, and no one with whom to discuss them. As much as he tried to dismiss the episode as some inexplicable hallucination, the missing hours as a freakish, one-off event, brought on, perhaps, by too much time spent near the heat of the blacksmith's furnace, he was never able to shake off the belief that even when offered the chance to save himself—and all of his loved ones—from a lifetime of suffering, he had blown it.

Depa sank into a depression so deep that it was all he could do to drag himself from his bed each day. His every action seemed ultimately futile. His life felt without purpose. Withdrawing into himself further and further, his sole, narrow focus became the money he earned working at the blacksmith, which was needed to provide for his family. If he didn't have to provide for them, he sometimes thought, he might just as well walk into the sea.

Several years passed, then one day a customer came to the black-smith to order the most elaborate and beautiful wrought iron ornamentation that had ever been commissioned. The work was to adorn two, arched doors that were gifts to a woman in a nearby village. The more that the customer spoke about the woman, the more extraordinary she seemed.

She made no claims to be a healer, said the customer, but she had given advice to many which had helped them recover from pain and suffering. She didn't call herself a spiritual teacher, but seemed to understand the hearts and minds of those who sought her help, offering the wisdom they needed to fill their lives with purpose.

What's more, her advice wasn't confined to the transcendent. Her savvy, commercial proposals had helped many around her grow rich, including the customer himself. It was as a token of his appreciation that he was ordering two magnificent doors that would form the entrance to a new home that he and other grateful villagers were building for her.

It was left to Depa to deliver the wrought ironwork, by ox cart, when it was completed a few weeks later. When his boss gave him the name of Maria Tilopa, it sounded vaguely familiar.

"You delivered a pair of iron hinges to her many years ago," said his boss, who never forgot a customer. "That was before—" he gestured to the cart, laden with fine ironwork, and the story that accompanied it "—all this."

Depa arrived at the new home being built for Mrs. Tilopa, and helped offload the ironwork to an area where the carpenter was already fashioning a pair of grand, front doors. After allowing the oxen a chance to drink from a nearby stream, he was about to return to work when, who should appear under the trees nearby, than the lady of the house herself. Depa took in the woman's homely figure and brilliant, turquoise eyes. He recognized her instantly as the person he had seen hurrying to the beach on the island of jewels, soon after he'd arrived.

But would she recognize him?

They exchanged formal greetings.

Depa reflected how the woman seemed, at once, both ordinary and extraordinary. Most of all, he felt touched by her presence of kindness.

"We have seen one another before," she said.

"Many years ago," he agreed, nodding. "I brought ironwork to your previous home. Hinges."

"I was thinking about the more recent occasion." She regarded him closely.

"The island of jewels?" It was the first time he had even uttered the words.

She nodded.

"I didn't know if you would recognize me from there."

"It was the most extraordinary blessing, was it not?" Her eyes sparkled with gratitude.

Depa looked at the ground.

"You don't think so?" Her tone was sympathetic—but there could be no mistaking her surprise.

"Unlike you, I didn't try to collect jewels until it was too late."

She nodded. "I remember you repairing bicycles."

"For four hours. Then I went to Trance Cove where I wasted all afternoon."

"Oh well," she said cheerily. "I expect you got the message, loud and clear, when it all came to an end."

For one who seemed so kind, and who had a reputation of possessing such great insight, the woman's attitude was insensitive, thought Depa. Callous, even. Yes, she had done the right thing on the island, but that was no reason to lord it over him, when he had come back with nothing. All the same, there was a question he *had* to ask her, one that had been burning inside him, destroying his peace of mind, devouring whatever small contentment he may have found for the past several years. It was a question that only an ascetic who had visited the island of jewels could possibly answer.

"Was it true, the rule about being able to bring home the jewels you found from the island?" he asked.

"I'm sure it is," she replied.

It seemed a strange answer. A confirmation, thought Depa, but not a direct one. Only because he was so desperate for certainty, he decided to risk offence by pressing the point. "When you came back, did you bring back all the jewels you had collected?"

She chuckled merrily. "Of course not! We can't carry physical objects with us from one state of mind to another."

Relief flooded through Depa. It was as if the gut-tightening, misery-inducing, self-recrimination of several years was suddenly released, in a palpable wave through his body. He felt suddenly liberated from the heaviest of burdens that had been grinding him down, day after day without reprieve. But along with the relief came confusion.

"So," he confirmed, "it wouldn't have made any difference if I'd spent all day collecting jewels?"

"I wouldn't say that exactly," she replied, gently. "It was the *collection* of precious jewels, remember, that we could bring with us. The act of collecting them has an impact on the mind. And the mind is all that travels from one state to another."

Depa understood the point that the woman was making. The same point made by the old man for whom he had bought the meal. The jewels themselves had no intrinsic value. It was the act of collecting them that made them precious.

"You are probably the only person around here who would understand what I mean when I say this—" the woman took a step closer to him "—but that vision we shared has changed my life. In the best possible way."

"It changed my life too," he agreed, bitterly, "but for the worst!"

"How so?!" she exclaimed.

"Because I came back empty-handed!" he cried. "I had no hope to offer my mother, my wife, my children! Nothing for my brothers and sisters, for any of the people I love."

"On the contrary, you have *everything*!" she protested.

Depa looked at her as if she was crazy.

It was only then that the woman realized. "Oh dear! You poor man." She took his hand between hers. "You have been thinking that the island of jewels is the place you went in our vision?"

"Was it not?"

"That you can never return?"

"I could?"

"That nothing you do here makes any difference because you have …"

"… blown it," he finished for her.

Maria Tilopa stood there, holding his hand, sending all the love and compassion that she could communicate from her own heart into his until, after the longest time, he looked up to meet her eyes.

"My friend, what we experienced was only a dream. A vision. *This* is the island of jewels. We are living on it! During our time here on earth we can choose to focus on material things alone, or we can make the cultivation of our mind and heart a priority. We can seek only to satisfy our short-term needs and gratify our senses. Or we can also give our attention to collecting the jewels of love and compassion, of generosity and ethics, of mindfulness and equanimity. For these are the only things we take with us.

"It doesn't matter if you are a blacksmith. I am a humble widow, well past middle age and not blessed by an attractive appearance. Even so, I have discovered that when I focus my attention on the things that endure, I experience wealth of an altogether different order. Peace which cannot be found elsewhere.

"I know many wealthy people who lack contentment, because it is a quality, a precious jewel, that has nothing to do with money. One we must cultivate for ourselves. And, the most curious thing is that others love us when we do. They can sense our benevolence and in their eyes we acquire a kind of beauty. We come to fulfill the two great purposes of helping both ourselves as well as others. *That* is the meaning of the island of jewels!"

When Depa returned home that evening he was a man unburdened. Lightness filled his heart and his mind was firm with purpose. Even the way he walked towards the family gathering was different.

"Let's all go down to the beach tonight to watch the moon rising over the ocean!" he suggested to where they were gathered in a circle around the embers.

They looked up at him in surprise. Trips anywhere were rare—mainly because he was always so tired.

"I'm sorry I've been such a misery to live with," he told them. "And I wish I had money to buy us all dinner at one of the fancy restaurants there. But I can give you my time and, for the moment, I hope my wish for your happiness is enough."

His three children leapt to their feet. From the corner, on the burlap sacks, his mother stopped groaning.

His wife, Leila, took his hand in hers and, for the first time in weeks, gazed him directly in the eyes and smiled. "It is enough."

THE FOUR IMMEASURABLES

(Love, compassion, joy and equanimity)

May all beings have happiness and
the causes of happiness.

May all beings be free from suffering and
the causes of suffering.

May all beings never be parted from the happiness
that is without suffering.

May all beings abide in peace and equanimity,
their minds free from attachment, aversion and free
from indifference.

Read the first chapter of

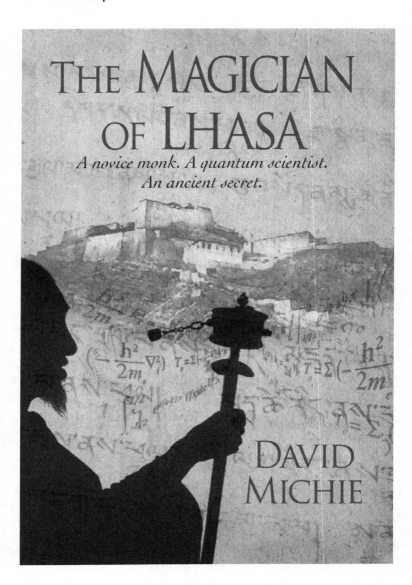

THE MAGICIAN
OF LHASA
A novice monk. A quantum scientist.
An ancient secret.

DAVID
MICHIE

THE MAGICIAN OF LHASA

CHAPTER ONE

Tenzin Dorje (pronounced Ten-zin Door-jay)

Zheng-po Monastery, Tibet
March 1959

I AM ALONE IN THE SACRED STILLNESS OF THE TEMPLE, LIGHTING butter-lamps at the Buddha's feet, when I first realize that something is very wrong.

"Tenzin Dorje!" Startled, I turn to glimpse the spare frame of my teacher, silhouetted briefly at the far door. "My room. Immediately!"

For a moment I am faced with a dilemma. Making offerings to the Buddha is considered a special privilege—and as a sixteen year old novice monk I take this duty seriously. Not only is there a particular order in which the candles must be lit. Each new flame should be visualized as representing a precious gift—such as incense, music and flowers—to be offered for the sake of all living beings.

I know that nothing should prevent me from completing this important rite. But is obedience to my kind and holy teacher not more important? Besides, I can't remember the last time that Lama

Tsering used the word "immediately." Nor can I remember a time when anyone shouted an order in the temple. Especially not Zheng-po's highest-ranking lama.

Even though I am only half way through lighting the candles, I quickly snuff out the taper. Bowing briefly to the Buddha, I hurry outside.

In the twilight, disruption is spreading through Zheng-po monastery like ripples from a stone thrown into a tranquil lake. Monks are knocking loudly on each other's doors. People are rushing across the courtyard with unusual haste. Villagers have gathered outside the Abbot's office and are talking in alarmed voices and gesturing down the valley.

Slipping into my sandals, I gather my robe above my knees and, abandoning the usual monastic code, break into a run.

Lama Tsering's room is at the furthermost end, across the courtyard and past almost all the monks' rooms, in the very last building. Even though his status would accord him a spacious and comfortable room directly overlooking the courtyard, he insists on living next to his novices in a small cell on the edge of Zheng-po.

When I get to the room, his door is thrown open and his floor, usually swept clean, is scattered with ropes and packages I've never seen. His lamp is turned to full flame, making him look even taller and more disproportionate than ever as his shadow leaps about the walls and ceiling with unfamiliar urgency.

I've no sooner got there than I turn to find Paldon Wangmo hurrying towards me. The pair of us are Lama Tsering's two novices but we have an even stronger karmic connection: Paldon Wangmo is my brother, two years older than me.

We knock on our teacher's door.

Lama Tsering beckons us inside, telling us to close the door behind us. Although the whole of Zheng-po is in turmoil, his face shows no sign of panic. Though there is no disguising the gravity of his expression.

"I only have time to tell you this once, so you must please listen carefully," he looks from one to the other of us with a seriousness we only see before an important examination.

"This is the day we have feared ever since the year of the Metal Tiger. Messengers have just arrived at the village with news that the Red Army has marched on Lhasa. His Holiness, the Dalai Lama, has been forced into exile. A division of the Red Army is traveling here, to Jangtang province. At this moment they are only half a day's travel from Zheng-po."

Paldon Wangmo and I can't resist exchanging glances. In just a few sentences, Lama Tsering had told us that everything about our world had been turned upside down. If His Holiness has been forced to flee from the Potala Palace, what hope is there for the rest of Tibet?

"We must assume that the Red Army is coming directly towards Zheng-po," Lama Tsering continues quickly. From outside we hear one of the women villagers wailing. "If they travel through the night, they could arrive by tomorrow morning. *Definitely*, they could get here within a day.

"In other parts of our country, the army is destroying monasteries, looting their treasures, burning their sacred texts, torturing and murdering the monks. There's little doubt they have the same intentions for Zheng-po. For this reason, the Abbot is asking us to evacuate."

"Evacuate?" I can't contain myself. "Why don't we stay and resist?"

"Tenzin Dorje I have shown you the map of our neighbor China," he explains. "For every soldier they have sent to Tibet, there are ten thousand more soldiers ready to take their place. Even if we wanted to, this is not a struggle we can win."

"But-"

Paldon Wangmo reaches out, putting his hand over my mouth.

"Fortunately, our Abbot and the senior lamas have been preparing for this possibility. Each of the monks has a choice: you can return to your village and continue to practice the Dharma in secret. Or you can join the senior lamas in exile."

He holds up his hand, gesturing we shouldn't yet reply. "Before you say you want to join us in exile, you must realize this is not some great adventure. Traveling to the border will be dangerous— the Red Army will shoot dead any monks trying to leave. Then we must try to cross the mountains on foot. For three weeks we will have to travel very long distances, living off only the food we can carry. We will have to endure much hardship and pain. Even if we finally arrive in India, we don't know if the government will allow us to stay, or will send us back over the border."

"But if we return to our villages and continue to wear our robes," interjects Paldon Wangmo, "the Chinese will find us anyway, and punish our families for keeping us."

Lama Tsering nods briefly.

"If we disrobe, we would be breaking our vows." Paldon Wangmo has always been a sharp debater. "Either way, we would lose you as our teacher."

"What you say is true," Lama Tsering agrees. "This is a difficult decision even for a lama, and you are novice monks. But it
is important that you choose, and do so quickly. Whatever decision you make," he regards each of us in turn, "you will have my
blessing."

From outside comes the pounding of feet as people hurry past.
There can be no doubting the crisis we're facing.

"I am now an old man, seventy four years of age," Lama Tsering
tell us, kneeling down to continue packing a leather bag which is
lying on the floor. "If I had only myself to think about, I might go
into hiding and take my chances with the Chinese-"

"No lama!" I exclaim.

Next to me, Paldon Wangmo looks sheepish. He has always
been embarrassed by my impetuosity.

"But the Abbot has asked me to play an important part in the
evacuation."

"I want to come with you." I can hold back no longer, no
matter what Paldon Wangmo thinks.

"Perhaps you like me as a teacher," cautions Lama Tsering. "But
as a fellow traveler it will be very different. You are both young and
strong, but I may become a liability. What happens if I fall and
hurt myself?"

"Then we will carry you across the mountains," I declare.

Beside me Paldon Wangmo is nodding.

Lama Tsering looks up at both of us, an intensity in his dark
eyes I have seen only on rare occasions.

"Very well-" he tells us finally. "You can come. But there is one
very important condition I have to tell you about."

Moments later we are leaving his room for our own, having prom-
ised to return very quickly. As I make my way through the turmoil
in the corridor outside I can hardly believe the condition that Lama
Tsering has just related. This is, without question, the worst day in
the existence of Zheng-po, but paradoxically for me it is the day I
have found my true purpose. My vocation. The reason I have been
drawn to the Dharma.

Opening my door, I look around the small room that has been
my world for the past ten years; the wooden meditation box, three
feet square. The straw mattress on the baked earth floor. My change
of robes, and toiletry bag—the two belongings we are allowed at
Zheng-po.

Not only is it hard to believe that I will never again sit in
this meditation box, never again sleep on this bed. It is even more
incredible that I, Tenzin Dorje, a humble novice monk from village
of Ling, have been accorded one of the rarest privileges of Zheng-po.
More than that—one of the most important tasks of our entire
lineage. Together with Paldon Wangmo, and under the guidance of
my kind and holy teacher, we are to undertake the highest and most
sacred mission of the evacuation. It means that our flight from Tibet
will be much more important—and more dangerous. But for the
first time ever I know, in my heart, that I have a special part to play.

My time has come.

Matt Lester

Imperial Science Institute
London
April 2006

I'm sitting in the cramped cubby-hole that passes for my office, late on an overcast Friday afternoon, when my whole world changes.

"Harry wants to see you in his office," Pauline Drake, tall, angular and not-to-be-messed with, appears around the door frame two feet away. She looks pointedly at the telephone, which I've taken off its cradle, before meeting my eyes with a look of droll disapproval. "Right away."

I glance over the paperwork strewn across my desk. It's the last Friday of the month, which means that all timesheets have to be in with Accounts by five. As Research Manager for Nanobot, it's my job to collate team activities, and I take pride in the fact that I've never missed a deadline.

But it's unusual for Harry to dispatch his formidable P.A. down from the third floor—and with such an absolute demand. I can't remember the phrase "right away" being used before.

Something must be up.

A short while later I'm getting out from behind my desk. It's not a straightforward maneuver. You have to rise from the chair at forty five degrees to avoid hitting the shelves directly above, before squeezing, one leg at a time, through the narrow gap between desk and filing cabinet. Then there's the walk along a rabbit's warren of corridors and up four flights of a narrow, wooden staircase with its unyielding aroma of industrial disinfectant and wet dog hair.

As I make my way across the open plan section of the third floor, I'm aware of being stared at and people whispering. When I make eye contact with a couple of the HR people they glance away, embarrassed.

Something's definitely up.

To get to the corner office, I first have to pass through the anteroom where Pauline has returned to work noiselessly at her computer. She nods towards Harry's door. Unusually it is open. Even more unusually, an unfamiliar hush has descended on his office, instead of the usual orchestral blast.

When I arrive, it's to find Harry standing, staring out the window at his less-than-impressive view over the tangled gray sprawl of railway lines converging on Kings Cross Station. Arms folded and strangely withdrawn, I get the impression he's been waiting specially for me.

As I appear he gestures, silently, to a chair across his desk.

Harry Saddler is the very model of the Mad Professor, with a few non-standard eccentricities thrown in for good measure. Mid-fifties, bespectacled, with a shock of spiky, gray hair, in his time he's been an award-winning researcher. More recent circumstances have also forced him to become an expert in the area of public-private partnerships. It was he who saved the centuries-old Institute—and all our jobs—by doing a deal with Acellerate, an LA based biotech incubator, just over a year ago.

"A short while ago I had a call from L.A. with the news I've been half-expecting for the past twelve months," he tells me, his expression unusually serious. "Acellerate have finished their review of our research projects. They like Nanobot," he brushes fallen cigarette ash off his lapel. "They *really* like Nanobot. So much that they want to move the whole kit and caboodle to California. And as the program originator and Research Manager, they want you there too."

The news takes me completely by surprise. Sure, there've been visitors from the States during the past year, and earnest talk of information exchange. But I never expected the deal with Acellerate to have such direct, personal impact. Or to be so sudden.

"They're moving very quickly on this," continues Harry. "They want you there in six weeks ideally. Definitely eight. Blakely is taking a personal interest in the program."

"Eight weeks?" I'm finding this overwhelming. "Why do I have to move to California at all? Can't they invest in what we're doing over here?"

Harry shakes his head in weary resignation. "You've seen the new shareholder structure," he says. "As much as Acellerate talk about respecting our independence, the reality is that they hold a controlling interest. They call the shots. They can strip what they like out of the institute and there's really not a lot we can do to stop them."

I'm not thinking about Acellerate. I'm wondering about my girlfriend, Isabella. She's more important to me than anything else in the world and after three years of working long and hard for Bertollini, the drinks manufacturer, she's just been promoted to Group Product Manager. The idea of her leaving her new job is a non-starter and there's no way I'm leaving her behind in London, no matter how great the interest of the legendary Bill Blakely.

Harry mistakes the cause of my concern. "If you look at what's happened to the other research programs Acellerate have taken to LA," he reassures me, "they've gone stratospheric." Pausing, he regards me more closely for a long while before querying in a low voice, "Isabella?"

"Exactly."

"Take her with you!"

"It's not that simple. She's just been promoted. And she's close to her family."

"A girl like her," Harry has met her at institute functions over the years, "she'll get a job like that in Los Angeles," he snaps his fingers. "And you'll be giving her family a good excuse to visit Disneyland."

As always, Harry is trying to keep focused on the positive. I understand, and I'm all the more appreciative because I know how hard this must be for him. Nanobot has always been one of his favorites. It was Harry who brought me into the institute when he discovered the subject of my Masters thesis. Harry who nurtured the program through its early stages. He and I enjoy a close relationship—more than my boss, he's also my mentor and confidante. Now, just as the program's starting to get interesting, he's having it taken off him. What's more, who's to say it will end with Nanobot? It seems that Acellerate can cherry pick whatever they like from the institute and leave Harry with all the leftovers. Small wonder he's in no mood for the Three Tenors.

"You really must see this as the opportunity that it is," he tells me. "With Acellerate behind you, you can accelerate the program way beyond what we can afford here. You could get to prototype stage in two, three years instead of seven or eight. With positive early tests the sky really is the limit. You'll be working at the heart of nanotech development for one of the best-funded scientific institutes on earth. Plus you'll even be able to catch a sun tan. Think of this as a great adventure!"

His phone rings, and we hear Pauline answering it outside. Evidently Harry has told her we aren't to be disturbed—something he's never done before.

There's another pause before I finally say, "I guess whatever way you package it, I don't have much choice do I? I mean, Acellerate aren't going to leave the program in London just because my girlfriend has changed jobs. And if I walk away from it, that's the last seven years of my life down the tubes."

He doesn't answer me directly, which I take as confirmation. Instead he says, "Look at me, Matt. Fifty four years of age. A little battle-wearied, a little scarred. But I've had my fifteen minutes in the spotlight. If it was just about me, I wouldn't have bothered trying to find a new partnership for the institute last year. I'd have just taken my chances with Government funding and hoped for the best."

I swallow. Harry has never spoken so directly to me before and I find his modesty humbling.

"But the Institute's not just about my ego or anyone else's. It's about the work we do. The science. All our research programs have the potential to transform peoples' lives. And of all the programs we're running," he regards me significantly, "*yours* is the most likely to make the most revolutionary impact."

I regard him closely.

"You're the first cab off the rank, Matt. It's flattering that Acellerate are so keen to take you off us. You're thirty four years old and this kind of opportunity doesn't come along often."

"It's a bit sudden, that's all," I'm nodding. "I mean, ten minutes ago, my main concern was getting the time sheets in."

Harry regards me with a look of benevolent expectation.

"I'm sure I'll get used to the idea."

"Good."

"I'll have to speak to Isabella."

"Of course." Harry reaches into a desk drawer, taking out a large white envelope which he hands me across the desk.

"Before you make up your mind, you might like to study the terms and conditions," he says.

A short while later I'm heading back to my office in a daze. Not only is Harry's announcement life-changing, the conditions of my appointment are way beyond anything I could have imagined. Almost too much to believe.

As I return through HR, I'm so preoccupied I don't notice anyone. Even the reek of the stairs passes me by. I'm trying to get my head around the paradox that this is terrible news for the Imperial Science Institute, but an amazing opportunity for me. That Isabella is almost certain to be upset by the same thing that is a personal endorsement beyond my wildest dreams. I hardly know what to make of it.

I return to the poky office which has been my home for the past seven years. The bulging shelves and worn metal filing cabinets.

The tiny desk swamped with paperwork. It's hard to believe I might be about to leave this all behind. That I have, in my hands, an extraordinary offer that could change my life.

Our lives.

I have to speak to Isabella.

Chapter One of *The Magician of Lhasa* by David Michie, Copyright ©2017 Mosaic Reputation Management (Pty) Ltd, Australia.

Excerpt used with permission.

ABOUT THE AUTHOR

DAVID MICHIE IS THE AUTHOR OF A *THE DALAI LAMA'S CAT* SERIES of novels, as well as non-fiction titles including *Buddhism for Pet Lovers, Why Mindfulness is Better than Chocolate, Hurry Up and Meditate* and *Buddhism for Busy People.* His books are available in 26 languages in over 40 countries.

In 2015 David founded Mindful Safaris, leading groups to Africa—where he was born and brought up—for journeys which combine game viewing with guided meditations. As the many returning members of the Mindful Safari family testify, these extraordinary experiences help us reconnect with nature, as well as with ourselves, in a relaxed yet powerful way.

www.davidmichie.com

Made in the USA
San Bernardino, CA
26 November 2018